I0662331

Boomerang
Bandito

Bob Longo

Copyright © 2019 Bob Longo
All rights reserved

ISBN: 978-0-578-49380-0

Thanks to Laurie, for her patience and sense of humor about all things, but especially me.

To Sharon Rosen, for making my words flow better than I could have done without her. To Marina and Jason for making them fit nicely on these pages.

To "Mo" Mobarick Abdullah for designing a beautiful and unique cover, to Pascale for connecting us, and to Michelle Ganeles for making sure it looks awesome in all its printed and digital lives.

Speaking of awesome, thanks to Nick, for taking a photo that makes me feel like a Florida author.

And to Brian, for being there. Always.

This is a work of fiction. All the names and characters are either invented or used fictitiously. Unless of course, if you care to think differently.

Boomerang Bandito

Part One

Chapter 1

Miami Beach, Florida. July 1982. It's early in the morning and I'm standing naked in a bathtub inside the New Yorker Hotel with a razor in one hand and a can of Nair in the other. I've done the best I can to not cut chunks of flesh from my body, but the combination of shaving and nairing, with the addition of the warm water coming out of the shower head makes me feel like hot, flaming matches are cascading off my raw body. Up until fifteen minutes ago, I was a very hairy young man. My name is Dan. Dan Griffin.

The painfully clean, bare look isn't a passing fancy I've designed to help me pick up models on South Beach, strolling bare-chested. No. It's so the duct tape can hold specially wrapped, tightly packed kilos of Columbian cocaine to my skin underneath a Body Glove wet suit, which itself is underneath khakis and a loose-fitting shirt and blazer. It's so the packages will stay put and stay unnoticed at the airport and on the plane. It's so when it is time to rip the duct tape and cocaine from my skin, my skin remains attached to my body, so I don't collapse in a crying, bleeding, whimpering mess in front of men with guns who would laugh, then likely shoot. And then I wouldn't be able to trade those very bad men all those neatly wrapped packs of cocaine for a duffle bag full of crisp, bundled, hundred-dollar bills later today in Colorado. No pain, no gain.

This is not the first time I have done this, nor I thought standing there, would it be my last. Between June and September, I have shaved and naired more than several dozen times. Each time I follow a now choreographed dance, dusting off with talcum powder and duct taping exactly twenty-two pounds of cocaine to my body. Forty-four small, half-pound plastic wrapped goodie bags that added up to ten kilos and a whole lotta money. It sounds like and is in fact, a lot of stuff taped to my body. It also sounds like it would be impossible to keep anyone from noticing the obvious bumps and bulkiness of it all. But therein was the amazing trick. Done right, it was virtually impossible to detect. At least back in 1982.

That summer, all in all, I did the duct tape trick upwards of fifty times. Each trip netted me twenty-five thousand dollars. Do the math, and you instantly understand why someone like me—a nice 19-year-old, catholic-school educated kid from the suburbs— working on a college degree in business, would risk jail or a quick, violent death doing something as foolish and dangerous as running drugs.

Money. Lots of it. Over a million dollars for shaving my body, flying around the country, remaining calm and acting cool. Looking back, it was quite an amazing feat not getting busted. So was not getting killed and dumped down a Colorado mountainside or left to rot in some watery hole in the Everglades. My skin was smooth, red and raw, but I was alive, happy and naïve. And yes, I was rich beyond my dreams. But of course, good things like that never last. They always get fucked up. You just never see it coming, even if you are constantly on edge waiting for it.

I hear a quick double knock on the hotel door followed by the turning of a key before it opens. In the insane coke and gun-filled world in which I lived that summer, knocking before opening a door, regardless of whether the door was open or unlocked, you had a key or not, was what you did. You never wanted to surprise someone. Surprises were bad.

Julie steps in, all suntanned, glistening and beautifully blonde, leggy and lithe.

"Hey, you getting ready?" she asks, knowing the drill as well as I do.

"Yeah."

"Good. Now rinse that shit down the drain so I can get in and get ready. We meet the boys in an hour."

Julie and I had been dating for about a year. We'd been running drugs for the past three months. We were a good match. Unique and identical senses of humor and danger greased the skids for our wild rides through the foolishly joined worlds of Columbian cocaine manufacturers, Cuban drug lords and Colorado yuppie money.

She was five foot two, 110 pounds, athletic, smart, funny, sensual and sexy. And most important to the task at hand— inside airports, she could instantly turn into the girl next door with girlish good looks and awe shucks smiles that always wooed security guards and cops. Equally advantageous, she could turn on a tough-as-nails cool aloofness that kept the baddest bad asses guessing. But to me, at least back then, Julie was a soul mate. Someone I could be myself with under any and all circumstances. Someone who knew my heart and mind as well as, if not better than, me. And the best part was, she felt the same way about me.

Maybe it was because she came from the same middle-class, Catholic school upbringing I did. We weren't brought up in the slums or a ghetto where drugs and drug dealing were a way of life, survival and getting ahead. We didn't need this world we lived in. We were good kids. Just a little bored and looking for fun, adventure, and a world foreign to us—but interesting enough to lure us in and keep us busy and happy. At least until something newer, cooler, and more adventurous came along.

Julie turned toward me to check and see how I was getting along. "Come on hairy nairy, move your cute little ass and maybe we can have a little play time before we get outta here and meet the boys."

I had been toweling off, slowly. Each rub against my baby fresh skin with the towel nearly brought tears to my eyes. When the shaving and nairing was finished, little pinprick size spots of blood would bubble out of my skin, sometimes for an hour or more, never stopping until the talcum powder sealed it in. And even then, the dull, throbbing pain would stay with me for a couple hours.

I was acting like a pussy, making little girly moans and thinking about my pain while Julie stripped off her bikini and walked around, packing a small bag. Watching her move, all tan and strong and sexy, and flashing me glimpses of her shaved pussy made me think less and less about my skin and more and more about hers. She was petite but athletic. Her straight blonde hair fell on powerful shoulders. Her back and arms and legs were highly defined, but oh so feminine. Her breasts fit perfectly in my hands and her nipples loved to be touched, kissed and licked.

"I'm moving faster already, tiny hiny. Play time is very important to a happy, healthy mind."

"Yeah," she laughed. "And a stiff dick!"

Chapter 2

The "boys" were anything but. Well-armed, well-drugged, well-sexed and easily combustible, they always brought an air of unpredictability to any meeting. Three brothers from Cuba. They were all under thirty and part of the fabulously wealthy drug crowd that ran South Beach back then. Their money and influence helped build the place. Juan, Carlos, and Roberto Villa owned an ultra-modern, rehabbed three-story art deco hotel they converted into their personal playhouse on Ocean Drive directly across from South Beach Park. You could stare straight out past the park at the Atlantic from nearly every room. It should have been a calm, peaceful place, but it was often anything but. The all-night coke and sex fueled parties were legendary. So were the quiet pre-dawn gatherings in the first-floor garage/work space that saw some guests leave hog-tied, gagged, and crammed into the back of one of their Land Rovers never to be seen again. I'd witnessed both with my own eyes. Far too many times.

Their place was on the other end of Miami Beach, far from my little hair palace in the New Yorker, and it just as well might have been a world away. The New Yorker's pool was partially filled with greenish water so thick it looked like a swamp. The beach behind the hotel was home to thousands of sand crabs that would pop out and scare the living shit out of you if you were brave enough or drunk enough to try to take a sunny doze on a beach towel. Their otherworldly crawl-a-thon might as well have been part of a nature documentary.

Inside, there was no art or deco left in the old place I called home that summer. The lobby was dark and dank. It smelled of mold, and crusty old men shuffled across cracked marble floors that had been polished for the satin gowns of movie stars waltzing away vacations decades ago. The rooms had great views but were damp and home to all sorts of big flying bugs that kept you swatting in the night.

The Villa brothers couldn't understand why Julie and I would stay in such a dingy and dirty place, when we clearly had the funds to stay somewhere nicer. The guys thought it was so disgusting, they wouldn't come near the place. That fact alone was reason enough to stay, even if I could have afforded to buy it outright.

When we rolled up to their place that morning, Roberto was standing outside in the driveway, next to a stone fountain, smoking a hand-rolled Cuban cigar. More likely than not, he and his brothers had been up all night. He wore baggy white linen pants that rustled in the breeze like a ship's sail on the open sea. His pressed short sleeve shirt was completely unbuttoned. His smooth skin underneath was beaded with sweat, as if he had been hard at work just moments before. Which in fact, he had. And of course, that was bad news for the sad soul who no doubt spent the night tied to a chair being worked over by him and his brothers. Whomever it was had either come to an agreement or was at this very moment being packed into the back of a Land Rover.

"What chew dewing, mang?" Roberto shouted to us over the spray of the fountain in the romantic Latin accent he used rarely and only for effect as we got out of Julie's Escort. He followed it with the perfect English the nuns had taught him in grade school. "You're not supposed to be here for an hour." There was no smile.

Subtleties were not Roberto's specialty. The tone of his voice and the words he used were a clear sign to Julie and me that we were early and unwanted. And arriving early or late were—like surprises—things I avoided that summer of 1982. We stopped in our tracks, smiled and said almost at the same exact time, "We can grab a coffee and come back."

There was a long pause, Roberto took a slow pull off his cigar, exhaled a cloud of smoke and finally, after what seemed like minutes, flashed his wide, welcoming smile, "Nah, come, we're all family here, no?"

Sure, the dysfunctional, drug-dealing, murderous kind of family. And it was time for some family bonding.

As we walked up the stone driveway to him, Roberto exhaled another big, puffy blue cloud of smoke and smiled broadly. The sun had that early morning glow as it hung low over the ocean, the air was still, and hungry seagulls sang their songs to anyone who would listen. He clasped my hand, brought me in close and hugged me. He pulled back and stepped in toward Julie and gave her the same hug, but without the handshake, adding a tender kiss on her right cheek in its place.

"You always look so beautiful," Roberto said softly to her.

"That's my job," Julie smiled back.

"Yes, it is. Come inside. I believe we are ready for you."

The inside of the Villa house was all crisp, clean lines, bright colors, tile floors, leather furniture, and flowers. Vases of flowers filled every room. The scents were never overpowering but rather pleasantly pungent, giving the space an outdoors, fresh personality. The three of us walked in through the front door and wound our way to the enormous entertainment room that overlooked and connected to the outside pool area out back.

It was a room designed for pleasure, but Julie and I also knew it as a place to get down to business. It was here, surrounded by artwork, giant TVs, stereo speakers, a pool table, and plush leather sofas, that we worked as a group to inspect and wrap the cocaine into manageable packets that would then be duct taped to my body. The brothers helped with it all, except for the duct taping part. They would just watch in silent wonder as Julie tenderly and expertly made me one with the coke.

Juan and Carlos walked into the great room all smiles. They were quieter and outwardly more reserved than their brother, but just as comfortable and confident. Neither looked like they'd spent the night partying and then torturing some business associate. They greeted Julie and me with hugs and handshakes, just as Roberto had outside. It appeared that, as was typically the case, the business in the garage had ended in their favor.

"We are so sorry to have kept you waiting. We had a, ah…we had a disagreement with one of our business partners. Thankfully, he saw things our way quickly and we came to terms."

All three brothers exchanged quick glances and giggled boyishly. Roberto shook his head from side to side, smiling and mumbling, "Yes, thankfully for him."

Roberto threw his head back and let out a hearty belly laugh. It filled the room. Juan and Carlos looked at each other, still smiling, shaking their heads. Julie and I did the same. But while Juan and Carlos were likely thinking "that crazy brother of ours," Julie and I were thinking "that brother of yours is crazy."

Carlos motioned for us to come in and get our business started. "Come, let's pour a drink and get to work."

We watched as the three brothers emptied a suitcase and laid out mounds of white gold on a large mahogany pool table cover. It was the best use the pool table would ever see. The height and size of the table were just right, allowing us all to stand comfortably as we set to work evenly dividing the bounty.

Half the cocaine had already been stacked, cut, divided, weighed, and bagged. The brothers had had a busy night. Julie and I started in on our task as they finished theirs. Hardly a word was spoken while our two teams worked. The sounds of razor blades and knives sliding across the smooth mahogany—and duct tape being pulled and cut—were the only noises in the room for long stretches at a time. No one was sampling. There was no music or talking. There was no partying. This was work. And the job called for the meticulous weighing and packaging of their product for sale. It required those packages to be taped to my body in such a way so that I had free movement, and most importantly, so that those packages were both invisible and undetectable to the probing, curious eyes of airport security.

This was pre-9/11 and back then, there were no long security lines, no TSA, no random searches, no shoe removals. If you looked like a law-abiding citizen, you were treated like one. And Julie and I were sticklers about looking like law-abiding, young lovers, cute as button citizens. The Body Glove covered, talcum-powdered baggies were sealed tight from even the random police dog we'd occasionally see strolling the airport. These were the good old days of out-in-the-open drug smuggling. If you avoided the random luggage searches—which we did by keeping only clothes and toiletries in our carry-on bags, and if you had the balls, the looks and the connections, you stood to get rich in a hurry. That is, as long as you didn't get killed by your friends and associates—which was far from a sure thing.

When it was all taped to my body, I went to the bathroom and peed. Going to the bathroom was not an option for the next five hours or so. Talcum powdered up and clothed in only white briefs, I squeezed into the Body Glove suit. The fit was super tight but counter intuitively, I had relatively full movement of my arms and legs. I threw on some nice, loose-fitting khaki linen pants, a cotton undershirt topped with a long-sleeved shirt and a baggy suit jacket. Finished, only ninety minutes after we began cutting the coke up, I stood there in silence while the three brothers and Julie stood back and silently gave me the once-over.

"You've been eating too much, my man," said Juan smiling. "I think you've put on a few pounds." Everyone laughed in approval.

Chapter 3

It never ceased to amaze Julie how easy it was for us to maneuver through airports undetected with over a half million dollars' worth of cocaine strapped to my body. Once we had figured out our system, I didn't waste a lot of time wondering or worrying. The cops and security staff had their system and we had ours. And ours was a good system proven not to conflict with theirs. End of discussion.

However, I did spend a considerable amount of time wondering and worrying about the Villa brothers, their Columbian connection cohorts, and the cartel of rich sharks in Colorado who were just as shifty, dangerous, and unpredictable as the Cubans and Columbians. I never lost sight of the belief, no—the fact—that their mood, desire, or goals could change in an instant, rendering us worthless and dead to them. It didn't matter that some of them were yuppies who dressed and spoke and acted nice. They carried pistols and rode around with automatic rifles and grenades in their cars and had the same hair-trigger tempers I'd seen in the Villa garage. To make matters worse, they were almost always jacked up on coke; twitchy, jumpy, and emotionally unpredictable when Julie and I were dealing with them. And we were always in a situation where seriously bad things could happen.

As was our routine, Julie and I left her car in the airport lot. We'd be back for it in just over a day. We carried our overnight bags over our shoulders and walked hand in hand through the lot, the people movers, and airport terminal. We talked softly, laughed, kissed, and stopped for a chocolate croissant, which we shared as our tickets were inspected and stamped at the American Airlines counter. We made idle chitchat with the girl behind the counter and moved on to our gate. Basically, we acted as normal as possible. And acting normal was good enough cover to fly cocaine around the country in those days.

There was virtually no security as we know it today. While there were police in airports, security gates—like ticket counters—were manned by airline employees or private security hired by the airlines. They were trained to look for certain "red flag" behaviors. Our job was to avoid triggering any of those pesky red flags. Specifically, Julie's job was to make us look normal.

The ticket counter folks noticed tickets paid for in cash on the spot. Especially one-way tickets. They also noticed when you had lots of luggage you didn't care to have checked. Things like that made them write "CODE" on your ticket and escort you to a security area where real police tended to ask lots of questions, frisk you, and search your bags.

The checkpoint employees—also privately employed by

the airlines—assumed you weren't smuggling drugs because their crackerjack teammates at the ticket counter had passed you through. So they were only looking for folks who looked and acted like hijackers. Keeping knives and guns out of your luggage, speaking English, being clean cut and not sweating profusely or twitching a lot was typically enough to get you by them and on the plane. The talcum powder under my Body Glove and the AC on high on the drive over was usually enough to keep me cool. Thankfully, neither of us twitched a lot. We were good to go.

Chapter 4

My clothes smelled like smoke, but otherwise, there was nothing to remember from the flight from Miami to Denver. Smoking on domestic flights would still be legal for another eight years. Running coke had always been against the law, so I kept my bitching to myself.

Truth be told, not only did I avoid talking about my drug smuggling; I didn't even think much about the legality or morality of what I was doing that summer. I was nineteen, had a sexy, beautiful girlfriend, gobs of cash, and I told myself I could get out of the whole business whenever I wanted. I'd be able to go back to school or wherever I pleased. Just walk away, unscathed. I told myself that doing drugs was a decision being made by thousands of other people. My actions weren't forcing them into a life of depravity and addiction. They had already made those choices and were going to buy their coke someplace, regardless of what I did. My actions wouldn't have even been possible without their decisions to consume drugs. My actions were a result of their lifestyle—not the other way around. I was merely in the right place at the right time, carrying out a business solution. If it hadn't been me, it would have been someone else. I had no guilt, no sleepless nights, no doubts.

We checked in to a Holiday Inn near Stapleton Airport shortly before 2:00 p.m., right on schedule. Finding a hotel for this sort of transaction was like buying a house. Location, location, location. Being close to the airport was our one and only need. We simply needed to do the deal, repackage the money in a box and FedEx it to ourselves in Miami—then fly back in the morning, pick up the box and bring it to the Villas. They would then unpack the box, count the cash, and hand us each twenty-five thousand dollars, in hundreds, for what amounted to two days' work. In a few days, we'd do the drill again, only we'd fly a different airline and stay in a different hotel.

This meant our weekly "salary" was $50,000 each, and we earned another $1.1 million for the Villas. Tax free. Before you knew it, that kind of money added up to some pretty serious cash. Not a bad payday—until the day the Villas wanted more. And that day was today.

Julie and I had a nice little bank close to the New Yorker with a friendly manager who was more than happy to take our deposits—with a small gift—whenever we came in. In Miami in 1982, it wasn't all that difficult to find an arrangement like that. And it worked for everyone. It was nice, tidy, and easy. We kept the bulk of the money in a large safe deposit box and told ourselves someday soon we would take some money out and invest in something like land or property. We kept a joint checking account with about a

$10,000 for our day to day needs.

I stood in front of our hotel room window in Denver, looking out at the congested chaos of I-70 off in the distance as I tried to meditate and block out the pain. The Rockies, as if part of some backdrop painting, clung to the horizon. Jets were roaring in and out overhead, but to me, their engines sounded exactly like duct tape being ripped off my body. This unwrapping was unpleasant business. Thankfully by now, Julie was a pro with a soft touch and the task took only a fraction of the time as the wrapping, which kept my pain at the grunt stage, instead of scream level, and left my skin mostly intact.

By three-fifteen, with the coke tucked away in our room, we were all freshened up and sitting pretty in the lobby, chatting and waiting for Chris Harris to show. Chris was twenty-five, six feet, two inches tall, 190 pounds, blond-haired and handsome. He carried himself with a self-assuredness typical of successful men ten years older. He managed to never look out of place. Seemingly always dressed in jeans over cowboy boots, a black t-shirt and leather jacket, he had the ability to act natural and friendly around anyone, in any situation. He'd always show up with a couple of other equally easy-on-the-eyes, natural looking guys about the same age, height, and weight, and we'd all end up looking just like a bunch of old pals reconnecting.

But that was just for show. The real deal was that Chris was the main mover of high-grade coke in these parts. The building construction company he inherited from his dad was involved with dozens of projects around the Denver area, making it the ideal laundering vehicle for the millions of dollars he made selling his cocaine through Vail, Telluride, and Breckenridge—all stomping grounds for West Coast types who had too much money and time on their hands, but it seemed, never enough cocaine. The construction company alone made Harris millions in the booming Colorado economy, but what was the fun in that? He grew up spoiled and easily bored and would rather associate with other rich, spoiled, and bored yuppies and the beautiful girls who clung to them, instead of uptight old men in suits and working-class stiffs in Carhartt overalls.

Harris, like the Villas, had the ability to make you feel completely at ease in his presence. Like there was nothing out of place or threatening. That this was just another errand in a typical, busy day; like dropping off clothes to the cleaners and picking up last week's batch. But Julie and I knew that façade was veneer-thin and that his animalistic survival instincts would kick in in an instant if the slightest danger was palpable. There was something dead inside him. His emotions were permanently in the "off" position. He had no deep connection to anyone and we knew he could just as easily shake your hand as put a bullet in the back of your skull.

The "pals" he brought with him to our meetings were all ex-military and trained killers. As a group, they were wired; with darting eyes, lean muscles, and hands ready to pull the brand new, sleek, self-loading Glocks from their shoulder holsters tucked under their jackets and blast away at anyone who made the wrong move. Julie and I always made it a point to smile, talk calmly, and move slowly around them. We'd always managed a calm, cordial, speedy transaction, but we knew the type and the danger. And if Chris was anything like the Villas, he ran his outfit with an iron fist with absolutely no room for error, sloppiness, or carelessness. Offenders were punished swiftly and harshly.

At three-thirty p.m., precisely on time, Chris walked through the revolving door with two of his pals. He appeared as always, in his casual-man attire—jeans, cowboy boots, black t-shirt, and a dark brown leather jacket. He glanced at us and peeled off his dark shades and flashed a smile. Of the three, he was the only one carrying anything. A medium-sized, black, nondescript duffel bag hung from his left shoulder. Inside was $600,000 in $100 bills. Six thousand of them, all wrapped neatly in $10,000 bundles. We'd go upstairs where I would count it all while Chris tested the powder. The Villas were very clear—never come back with less than the agreed upon amount of cash or bad things would happen. Like leaving their South Beach mansion hog-tied and gagged in the back of a Land Rover on a one-way ride to the Everglades.

The group was memorable because of their good looks and athletic bodies, but equally forgettable because their clothes, actions and movements were not the least bit out of the norm. Just three regular Colorado guys meeting old friends who'd just flown into town. They strolled over to where Julie and I had come to meet them, in a sitting area in the corner of the lobby. We both got up.

"Hey Chris, how have you been?" I asked, sticking out

my hand, exactly as I had been doing in hotels around Stapleton Airport twice a week for the past three months.

"Oh man, it is SO good to see you! What a shame you guys can only stay the day," he answered back, on cue as he stepped in, shook my hand firmly, and clapped me on my back crisply with his free hand—for the second time this week.

Chris then looked over at Julie, stepped away from me and came in with a big warm smile and open arms, hugging her as he would the girlfriend of a friend he hadn't seen in a long while. "Jules, you look awesome as usual. How are you?"

"Aw, thanks," replied Julie with a bit of polite shyness in her body language.

"I'm great. You look terrific too. You never seem to change or get any older. You look exactly the same every time I see you."

There was no falseness to any of that. Standing next to each other, I noticed how Chris stood a full foot taller than Julie, dwarfing her petite body. His two pals were equally tall, lean, and strong. And while they were smiling at the scene playing out in front of them, their heads swiveled slowly from side to side as they scanned the lobby in a practiced routine, looking for the smallest sign of a threat or anything out of place.

It all would have seemed so perfectly normal to a casual onlooker, except of course that it wasn't. We were about to move upstairs to our tiny room and make our transaction. For a brief but painfully suspenseful ten to fifteen minutes, the drugs and the money would be together, like gasoline and matches, in the same small room. Chris and I would count cash and check the coke while Julie and the two thugs, no longer smiling, stared at each other uneasily. The smallest flinch or jumpy movement could spark a wildfire of emotion and violence. We hadn't had a deal go wrong yet, but the possibility that it could was always there in the back of my mind. For all of us really, but everyone acted calm, and we all played our parts to perfection each time just the same.

Julie and Chris took the lead as we walked toward the elevators and our room, keeping the pretense as they spoke. They talked innocuously about the weather and how it was perfect for lunch outdoors at a Washington Park Grille Chris liked to frequent. Julie agreed it was an ideal day for lunch in the sun. The talk was friendly and the pace the two men and I kept behind them was casual. Even so, out of habit, we all continually kept looking about for the slightest sign of danger or anything out of place. That's when I saw them.

The Villa brothers were typically dressed in loose fitting linens and silks, always looking the part of the well-to-do Latin businessman—and they played that part to perfection. Today, they were in different clothes and roles. Even though they came through the revolving front door in jeans, leather jackets, shades, and baseball caps with duffel bags over their shoulders, I recognized them instantly. They weren't the vacationing brothers and friends they portrayed. They were drug dealing killers on the prowl. The shock of seeing them here in Colorado nearly froze me dead in my tracks. My jaw dropped, but I somehow held back the guttural scream of terror that had immediately welled up inside of me. The sight of them, here in Denver, was something I had never considered. Not ever.

How did they get here? They had to have taken a charter. But how did they know where we were staying? How did they find us? Were we tailed? We never divulged the specific details of our trips going or coming to either the yuppie drug kings or the Cuban drug lords unless they were involved in the meet. And the Villas were never involved with the meet. They specifically avoided it. Yet here were the Villas, sauntering up to Chris and his muscle. I couldn't wrap my head around what I was seeing.

And in the seconds given to me to react, I couldn't wrap my head around what I should do about it. Were the Villas here to kill me and Julie and throw in with Harris? That seemed completely implausible. We were but mules—our entire role was to move their cocaine without the need or expense of pilots and planes—and bring back piles of money. They were the ones who decided we were needed— not the other way around. We kept them out of the dirty business of dealing directly with dealers like Chris, and as long as they always received the money they expected, the arrangement worked. And Julie and I never cut them short. Never.

Were they here to confront and kill Chris and his men? It seemed unlikely, but while the arrangement appeared by all accounts to be mutually beneficial, it was possible. The Villas were greedy, aggressive drug dealers after all, and if they sensed that they could take out the middle man here in

Colorado, they would increase their take by millions.

That had to be it. Instead of making $550,000 with each shipment, they could set up shop here in Colorado and sell their coke at retail—bypassing Chris and selling directly to his customers. But even if Julie and I weren't the targets, I knew the Villas wouldn't care if we were caught in the crossfire. They would simply replace us with two other mules. I had to make sure that didn't happen.

The thugs saw the brothers too as they strode through the lobby. Never having met them in person, they didn't recognize the Villas. And seeing how the three talked to each other jovially and innocently and looked like pals as they walked, they didn't give them a second glance. Even though they were headed straight for us, they didn't appear to present any danger. I knew better.

The brothers were talking, amazingly in near perfect English, about their expectations of the weekend wedding of their make-believe cousin. The conversation grew louder as they got closer. They laughed excitedly and spoke happily, yearning for the get together with family and friends. It was exactly the sort of conversation one might expect in a hotel lobby. They must have seen it in a movie.

Julie and Chris were stopped at the elevator with their backs to the Villas, waiting for the doors to open, still conversing casually, unaware of the Villas. My mind raced. I had lost track of what Julie and Chris were talking about. I only had ears for the Villas. I was listening and looking for a sign. Anything—a verbal cue, a nod, a look in my direction—anything I could take as an indication of what was to come. There was nothing. And that was a big problem. I had seen this Villa behavior at their house parties. One moment they were fun-loving, talkative, dancing, and happy. The next, they were spitting with rage, anger, and violence, waving pistols and threatening dismemberment and death.

I had done all I could to remain cool and calm on the outside, but on the inside, I was consumed by an all-encompassing fear. Getting on that elevator with Harris, his muscle, and the Villas could be the last thing I ever did.

We stood there waiting for the doors to open. All of us. After what seemed like an eternity, there was a loud "ding" and the doors began to pull back. That's when Julie saw the brothers, too. She had heard their loud conversation and was looking around to see who was doing all the talking. Juan looked right at her and gave her a wink. There was an almost imperceptible pause in her own fake discussion with Chris, but somehow, she too managed to keep it together. Now expressionless, she slowly turned her head toward me. Our eyes met and locked. It was, and remains the single most intense, all-communicating non-verbal look I have ever shared with another person. Our party was over. We both knew it. We were fucked.

Chapter 5

Without a "Plan B," Julie and I jammed inside the elevator with the others. There we were, all eight of us, $600,000 in cash and probably at least six handguns—a couple of shotguns and maybe a small Uzi sub-machine gun and a grenade or two—jammed inside a four-and-a-half by six-foot space. Chris and Julie were in the back, the two thugs and I were in the middle, and the Villas were in the front. Turning, looking past me and directly at Chris, Roberto asked casually, "Which floor?"

There was a pause. After a few seconds I heard Julie's voice, as if from in a dream, "Seven, thanks."

"Seven, ah, same as us." Roberto said, as he smiled and pressed the button.

"And a lucky number. Gonna have to play that on a lottery ticket tonight!" he added in perfect English.

The doors closed, and the elevator lurched upward.

Two. Still alive.

Three. No shots fired yet.

Four. Not a word spoken.

At five, Chris broke the silence.

"Vacation?" was all he said, asking it out loud to anyone who would answer. It was instinct to double check every interaction. Survival instinct.

"Wedding." The one-word, monotone answer came from Juan, who turned and looked Chris right in the eye as he spoke it in perfect English.

"Can't wait for the excitement to start," chimed in Roberto, smiling unthreateningly. Carlos, always quiet, said nothing. Perhaps Chris's senses were snapping like frayed electrical wires, but he showed no emotion. We all kept moving.

Six.

Looking back on it, my mind was both clear of thought and filled with fear. I had expected guns to be pulled and bullets to fly at any second.

Seven. The ride ended uneventfully.

The doors opened. Instead of gunfire and violence, everyone just sort of ambled out of the elevator quietly, the way folks normally do. Roberto was digging through his pockets, seemingly searching for his door key. I turned right, followed by the muscle, Julie and Chris. I heard an "Ah, here it is," from Roberto, who was still acting out his part to perfection, finally pretending to find his imaginary door key.

I walked down the hall to our room, put the key in the lock and opened the door. I held it open as I walked in. Julie had snuggled up directly behind me and put her hand on my back as I walked through the doorway. The physical connection would have to do. She had to replace all the words she no doubt wanted to say to me in that instant but was afraid to. She couldn't so much as utter a sound, so as not to act strange or out of the norm. She was as confused and concerned about the Villas' unexpected arrival as I was. But what could we do about it?

The two thugs followed us into the room. Chris was the last to enter. I stopped, turned, and as the door swung closed behind us, watched as the Villas—looking straight ahead and never glancing in—strolled nonchalantly by. Whatever they had planned, it was not going to happen here and now. Maybe they were going to ambush Chris after the deal or follow him and attack and interrogate him to find out the details of his network. Julie and I still had a chance to do this deal and get out of this room alive.

We were all bottlenecked in the tiny little hallway that led from the door past the bathroom and into the bedroom area. Inches from her as we moved ahead, I looked back at Julie and exchanged a look that said, *well, we're still alive*.

Let's do this and get the fuck out of here fast, is all I could think at that moment. Still in the room's hallway choke point, I turned my attention to Chris, looked him square in the eye and said, "Let's get this started."

We were interrupted by a harsh, loud, splintering sound, as the door was violently kicked off its hinges. The raw sound of it forced me to jump. My mind couldn't find a description for what was happening even though in my heart, I knew this was what the beginning of the end sounded like.

We all began to turn toward the noise in the same instant it erupted. I could see Chris and his thugs simultaneously reaching under their jackets for their guns as the door flew open, revealing the outlines of three men with guns pointed at us. I felt Julie's hand grip my shoulder as she exclaimed, "No!"

The next sounds were from Juan's always ready .44 Magnum. I'd seen him play around with it and clean it at the house back in Miami once, and thought to myself then that I never wanted to be staring down its giant barrel.

The shots from the .44 Magnum sounded more like canon blasts fired from three feet away than gunshots. There were three blasts—one after another after another—within a second or two. Blood, chunks of brain, scalp, and wisps of Julie's previously perfect blonde hair sprayed across my face and chest as her body catapulted into mine, knocking me down. The .44 had found its mark.

There were more gunshots in the next instant, five or six, maybe more, from different sounding guns. I couldn't see as I fell backward and tumbled into the room. Julie's blood blinded me. I still wasn't hit, but I heard the unmistakable sounds of bullets hitting flesh and bone. Bullets were finding their marks as even more shots were being fired. It appeared that everyone with a gun was using it. The noise was warlike and deafening. If words were being spoken, or screams being uttered, I could not hear them over the roar of the battle.

Two shotgun blasts rang out next. One of the thugs was falling backward and over me, still firing his Glock toward the door, expressionless with a giant, bloody hole in his chest. Something hot tore through my left forearm. There were a couple more blasts from the Glocks, the .44, and at least one more from a shotgun. Something hard and heavy hit me square in the back and I fell across Julie's body, and landed on the duffel bag filled with coke. Silence.

The gunshots appeared to have stopped. I couldn't hear anything over the very loud ringing in my ears. The awful smell of sulfur filled my nostrils and hung in the air. No one was left standing. No one.

Chapter 6

I thought I knew what shock would feel like. I'd certainly heard about it, read about it. I thought I knew what to expect, but I never imagined I'd have a death-defying firsthand experience with it. Not like this. I was physically and emotionally numb. I couldn't form any rational, coherent thoughts. And I couldn't hear. The sound of the jets flying in and out of Stapleton was lost in the hissy roar that rang in my ears from the gunshots. It was as if I were viewing the room and the world around me through someone else's eyes, with a bad soundtrack running in the background to boot. If only.

I felt a dull throb in my left arm. I raised it only to stare into what appeared to be a quarter-size hole in my forearm. A steady, bright red ooze flowed from the wound. Oddly, it didn't hurt as much as it looked like it should have. A bullet from one of the Glocks must have gone clean through. The shotgun would have left a wider field of damage and the .44 probably would have ripped my arm in two.

There was a lot of blood on and around me. There was red spray on the walls, furniture, and carpet everywhere I looked. The curtains blew in a breeze that came through the broken windows that had holes blasted into them. Even though I lay on top of her, Julie's left arm and leg were somehow draped over me in a pose lovers often find themselves in when waking in the morning. Or as it turns out, when one of them is dead, having caught a bullet in the head that would have otherwise struck the other. Her body lay entwined with mine, facing away from me. Still not accepting the reality sprawled out in front of me; I pushed my body up with my right arm and leaned up and over to get a better look at her, hoping she was merely injured, like me. I instantly regretted it. Her beautiful face was mostly gone. Her right eye, now lidless, stared lifeless at the wall. The bullet must have caught her square in the cheek, going through her head and blowing a hole clean through the back of her skull. Death had come and taken Julie in an instant, but I knew in that moment that I would carry the image of her murder, and the responsibility for it, with me forever.

Julie was dead. Dead. My first great love was gone in an instant. Gone. Forever. Even though we had lived in this crazy, dangerous world, we had naively assumed that we would easily navigate our way through it unscathed and exit happy and still young and playful on the other side. Untouched and alive. That's what we had told ourselves as we held each other at night in the hotel room purchased with drug money, and that's what we had believed in our hearts. What a fantasy. What a crock. How could we have been so foolish? This was always going to be how it ended.

I leaned back over and sat up. I began to make out the

sound of an alarm ringing non-stop somewhere in the distance over the ringing in my ears. I tasted an awful, metallic, sulfur taste in the back of my throat. Wisps of smoke hung and wafted about in the hotel room air, highlighted by the afternoon sunlight and wind coming through the windows. The curtains blowing in the breeze coming through the broken windows were the only things in the room moving. There was a pile of bodies strewn down the room's short hallway from where I now sat, stacked up out toward the door and the hotel hall. I was the only one moving. Half the bodies had their feet facing the hall, the other half had their feet facing the windows. It was as if a giant weight had fallen from the sky, landed square in the middle, and the shock wave blew them all backward to their deaths.

Chris's body and the bodies of his two thugs were lying at my feet, an entangled bloody mass of arms and legs. Each had been shot multiple times. It looked like pieces of hamburger were peeking through their shirts. One of the thugs stared upward, expressionless. His face from his nose down was gone. Gone. Chris looked as if he had been hit with several shotgun blasts to his chest—his clothes and skin were ripped open and his torso had dozens of holes in it.

This was war. A Villa power play, pure and simple. They'd schemed and surmised that they could catch the yuppies here, kill them outright, take their cash and sell the coke. Not just this once, but for evermore. They were eliminating the middle man. If Julie and I were eliminated too, then so be it. We were all replaceable.

I brought myself to my feet and stepped through the bodies, slowly working my way toward the doorway. Juan and Carlos had fallen on their sides and lay there back to back. Juan's .44 was in his left hand and he held a sawed-off shotgun in his right. Carlos only had one hand, which was still clutching a large handgun. His left arm, from the elbow down, was gone. It must have been hidden someplace beneath the gore. Both their bodies had been riddled with holes. They must have been face to face with the thugs, mere feet apart as they all unleashed waves of bullets at each other. Roberto was lying half in and half out of the doorway, face down. His magical smile and any bullet holes he now owned were hidden forever from my view. How had he so badly misjudged the yuppies firepower and quick reaction to his surprise assault? How was it that I had only been struck by one bullet?

The alarm was still ringing. And standing closer to the doorway, I realized just how loud it was. No one had showed up yet, but it was just a matter of time until police and a SWAT team was on scene sweeping floor by floor, room by room. Spending my life in jail was no more appealing than getting shot to death. I needed to get my shit together now and as cold as it seemed, put Julie and this unspeakable carnage I was a part of, out of my head and get the fuck out of here as fast as I could. Grieving would have to wait.

Fuck, fuck, FUCK!

OK, first things first. I had to wrap my arm and stop the bleeding. It didn't seem like a life-threatening, gusher of a gunshot—sure, this was my first time getting shot and all, and I was by no means an expert in these matters—but there just didn't seem to be enough blood, damage, or pain. Shit, I didn't even feel it yet, but that was probably because I was in shock or something fucked up like that.

The bullet, probably from one of the handguns, appeared to have gone through and through, leaving a clean hole straight through my forearm without hitting any veins or arteries. Considering the state of everyone else in the room, I was one fucking lucky drug dealer.

Trying not to look at Julie, I stepped through the bodies and into the bathroom and grabbed a couple of towels and wash cloths. A quick glance in the mirror told me I had better get the blood splatter off my pale face too. I stepped back through the dead and headed over toward our luggage, which was sitting undisturbed by the windows. Tearing and cutting the towels, I made quick work of a makeshift bandage, changed shirts, wiped down my face, arms and hands, and threw on a jacket. Only a few minutes had elapsed. I just might escape.

As much as I was racing to get out, and as cold-blooded as it may have seemed, it would have been foolish leaving without the cash. That $600 grand would come in handy in whatever future I would build if I got out of here alive. Besides, I told myself that it would probably "disappear" from a police evidence locker anyway. And the coke? Shit, I might as well take that, too. If I could get to Miami, I could figure out how to unload that for some cash. No one here was going to miss it.

I walked back through the fallen. The duffel bag, which

had been slung over Chris's shoulder, was lying amidst the bodies. It was covered in blood splatter and riddled with bullet holes. The strap had been ripped in two. I stepped in, leaned over and picked it up, half expecting Carlos's missing hand to be holding on to it. I weaved my way back through the carnage to the windows, emptied the bag, and packed the cash, coke, clothes, and toiletries together in my bag and slung it over my shoulder, then walked back through the bodies one final time. I stopped, bent over and picked up one of the Villa's baseball caps and put it on my head, covering any splatter there I may have missed. As I passed the full-length mirror, I stopped and looked at the pale, haggard, strange person staring back at me. I didn't recognize the man I'd become. This was not the carefree and happy 19-year-old I envisioned myself to be. The blank, hollow, emotionless expression on my face was haunting. Who had I become? It was another passing thought that would have to be tucked away and analyzed at a later date when I had more time to think.

From the hotel hallway, I gave one last look back at the life I'd known. The free spirited, high-flying, have it all world I'd been living in had crash landed here in this room. Everyone along for the ride except me was dead. I'd gone from effortlessly having it all to being alone, likely wanted by the police and with no real future, all in the span of a few minutes. From cocky and calm, to fearful and numb, and now to an awful, detached aloofness.

I took tight hold of the bag that held the ticket to my immediate future and possible salvation, and quickly and quietly scampered to the stairway. I ran down two flights of stairs and walked into another floor's hallway.

The alarms were ringing here too, and a few people were running hurriedly about. It was essential I looked like the rest of the panicked hotel guests. I figured I could take advantage of the chaos and mix in with the crowd, use them as a cover. I looked to see if I had a clear shot to the elevator to get to the lobby when a middle-aged woman bumped into me, grabbed my good arm and whispered in a fearful tremble, "Are the stairs clear? We heard there was a shooting on a top floor and I'm afraid to use the elevator."

"I think so, yeah," was all I could think to say.

She and a small group of others, some with bags, others with nothing but the clothes on their backs, wordlessly pushed past me and hurriedly began running down the stairs. Without the slightest hesitation, I joined in.

Seconds later we all burst out into a lobby that was a swarm of police, firefighters, movement, and noise. It seemed every cop in the room turned toward us with itchy trigger fingers and antsy nerves. Luckily, they all quickly came to the conclusion that we were a frightened mob of innocents fleeing the hotel, rather than fugitives trying to escape, and stood down.

I ran smack into a cop who was speaking calmly into his radio, "Yes sir, we are in the lobby, getting guests out of the building. The SWAT team is staging in the parking lot and almost ready to go in. We believe the gunfire came from one of the top floors. Fire and Rescue is here also." There was a pause and then he said, "No sir, we do not have a count on injured or dead."

I had hung back to eavesdrop on his conversation. He suddenly noticed me and said, "Whoa buddy, watch where you're going. You OK?"

"Ah, yeah," I said, barely able to mutter the words. "What the heck is going on? Someone said something about a shooting, so I grabbed my bag and headed downstairs."

"What floor were you on?" he asked, as he continued to scan the crowd.

"Three." I lied without hesitation, knowing from what he had said they were focused on the upper floors. Low floors meant I was just another fleeing guest. Anything higher and I could be viewed completely differently. Blending in was key to my survival.

"OK, make your way through the lobby to the parking lot. Someone will get to you in a few minutes."

How could he not read the lie in my eyes? Not see that moments ago I was scrubbing my girlfriend's blood and guts off of me?

"Thanks," was all I muttered, not looking him in the eye.

The hotel's sirens suddenly stopped. The surreal silence did nothing to ease the tense conditions, but it did at least make it quieter. People were scurrying around with quizzical expressions and aimless direction. All geared up and armed to the teeth with automatic rifles in hand and pistols strapped to their legs, the SWAT team was set, and with a unified grunt, ran into the building that everyone else was running from.

There were only a few cops left in the parking lot, and they were directing people leaving the hotel toward one of the fire trucks where paramedics were calmly talking and checking people over for injuries. Police commanders on scene must have somehow come to the false conclusion that the gunman or gunmen were still in the building, which gave me some breathing room.

I wasn't the only person who had dashed from the hotel with bags or luggage, but I was the only one with a bag full of cash and cocaine slunk over my shoulder. With as normal a gait, pace, and purpose as I could summon, I walked calmly past them all, through the parking lot and turned right, strolling to the hotel next door. From its circular drive, I became a normal traveler leaving a hotel, and flagged down a cab. I threw my bag in the back seat and calmly and slowly climbed in, asking the cabbie to take me to the Airport Marriot nearby. I would check in there, wash up, and get my head straight before I flew back to Miami later tonight or tomorrow.

Chapter 7

A short while later, for the second time in two days, I once again found myself in a hot shower and in pain, only this time I was wondering what I had gotten myself into instead of looking forward to the adventure I was about to embark on. Unlike yesterday, it wasn't my freshly shaven skin on fire, but rather, my head, my arm, and most of all, my heart. I was consumed with grief and felt heavy and broken by this afternoon's turn of events.

I had started my day with the love of my life by my side. Hours later, I was in the shower washing her blood, blonde hair and chunks of scalp from mine. While I had always been keenly aware of the danger that surrounded us in this deadly game we'd been playing for months, I was genuinely shocked by the dramatically sudden way in which death's hand had gripped Julie tight and held her, while only brushing me aside.

We had both steeled ourselves for as many potentially violent and deadly events as we could imagine, either at the hands of the Villa brothers in Miami, or by Chris or one of his minions here in Colorado. The Villas coming here for a slaughter that caught us all in a hellish blitzkrieg crossfire was never on the list of possible deadly fates we envisioned. As prepared as we thought we'd been, we were caught completely off guard and were utterly defenseless.

Standing, still dripping wet with a towel around me, I flipped on the TV. The breaking news crews were already on scene and reporting. They had a female—my Julie—listed among the unknown dead. No names were given, just a number. Six dead, the blonde reporter said breathlessly. Six? Further proof TV reporters were bubbleheads who were seldom right. There were seven bodies stacked in that hallway. I had seen them all with my own eyes, but I wasn't going to call asking for a correction.

"A pile of bodies, six in all, jammed into a tight, blood-filled hotel room hallway," the bubbly blonde spewed breathlessly. "All with multiple bullet wounds from what police sources tell me was a fast and furious gunfight. Five men and one woman. Nameless and dead. All indications here are that this was a drug deal gone bad."

No fucking shit, idiot. It didn't take the FBI to come to that conclusion.

"A blood trail through the hotel and out to the street leads police to believe that at least one other person, wounded in the hail of gunfire, likely made off with money, drugs or both."

Blood trail?

"Police dogs and a SWAT team are on the trail now. This entire area is on lockdown."

What the fuck? I bolted to the window and looked out,

the parking lot was devoid of police. What was this about a blood trail?

There was plenty of blood in that hotel room but there's no way that blood trail extended from that room through the hotel and out to the street. No way. Not from me. I'd bandaged my arm pretty well, with a tight seal that prevented any blood from seeping out. I'd made sure I had no blood or splatter on me and I wasn't dripping blood. I'd cleaned up, changed my clothes and wiped my feet thoroughly. I walked out the front door of that place as it was surrounded by cops and paramedics, and no one gave me a second glance. I had given the cab a good once over as I got out and it was clean too. When I got here and stripped down for this shower, my arm wound was still sealed tight. There was no "blood trail." Not from me.

This left several possibilities, and none of them were ideal.

First, the reporter was wrong. She'd simply gotten the information mixed up. Everyone knows TV reporters aren't rocket scientists.

Or, the police had lied to the reporter to cover up pertinent facts with the hope that they could trick those responsible for the shootings and that the bad guys would then somehow come forward or slip up, allowing them to fall in to a police trap.

The third possibility was the most troubling. And that was this; that the police had told the reporter the truth and there was in fact a blood trail leading from the crime scene.

And if that were the case, one of the dead bodies stacked

high in the hallway that I'd seen with my own two eyes, had gotten up and dragged itself out of that bloodbath and escaped.

But who? Who was still alive other than me?

Urgent and panicky thoughts now began to form one after another and run wild inside my head like a flickering silent movie as I stood there staring at the TV.

I'd seen the hole in Julie's head, held her dead face in my hands and had washed her blood from my own skin. As painful as it was to visualize this, it was the easiest piece of this puzzle to put in place. Julie was dead and gone forever and not limping through side streets with police bloodhounds on her trail.

I sat down on the edge of the bed and closed my eyes, picturing the scene as best I could, ignoring the desire to forever force it from my mind. Which one of those bodies was now up and walking around?

Once I concentrated fully, it didn't take long to deduce who that might be. Chris and his muscle were surely dead. Too many bullet holes and missing body parts in every one of them. Plus, I'd stared into their dead eyes. The same was true for Juan and Carlos.

This left Roberto. His was the last body I'd stepped over as I left that room. His was the only body that didn't have obvious fatal wounds and the only one I failed to thoroughly inspect.

Sure, he was lying face down in a pool of blood with what appeared to be multiple bullet holes in his back, but truth be told, I never really checked him over. I never turned him over to see if he was dead or alive. I just assumed he was dead, like everyone else in that pile, wrote him off and stepped over him. With *his* cash and coke in my bag.

Roberto could be alive. Fuck. Roberto, leader of the Villa drug empire, alive. Roberto, master manipulator and violent, sadistic torturer and murderer, alive after a failed bloody coup that left his brothers dead and mounds of his coke and cash missing. Fuck me.

If that indeed was the case and Roberto had taken his own headcount before dragging himself out of there, he would now know that his cash and cocaine were missing, and me along with it. He would realize that I had not checked on him, not tried to get him out of there, and that I had stolen his property. This was not good. Not good at all. He'd be angry beyond anything I'd ever seen before and he'd be laser focused on one thing: finding me, reacquainting himself with his drugs and money and setting things straight with me in a violent, final ending. It didn't matter that I didn't orchestrate the massacre. It only mattered that I had left him for dead and walked off with what I assumed was mine, but was in fact, *his*. I had stolen *his* goods. There was no greater sin in the Villa world. Fuck. Fuck. Fuck.

As if I wasn't already in a hurry to blow this town, this sealed the deal. I urgently needed to get out of here as fast as humanly possible and get back to Miami to get my own world in order. I'd sell the coke, take the cash from that sale plus what Julie and I had saved thus far in our escapades, leave town and head toward some out of the way place where I could begin the process of starting over.

It was crazy, and I was compounding the danger I faced by running from Roberto, but at this stage there was no turning back. He'd come for me regardless now and take the anger and pain he felt over his brother's deaths out on me.

Sure, a sane person would blame himself for being greedy and botching the ambush and would tell himself he got what he deserved and maybe slink off someplace, nurse his wounds and quietly start over. But these boys weren't sane. Especially Roberto. He would assume I had freaked out when I spotted him and his brothers in the lobby and that once the hotel room door had closed, that I had quickly and urgently cut some sort of deal with Chris, enabling him and his yuppies to fight back with such deadly ferocity. If it hadn't been for me, his attack would have been a cakewalk instead of a bloodbath that left his brothers dead. He would convince himself that not only had I stolen his goods, but I was a traitor to boot.

I'd need to find someplace off the grid that was completely out of his sight and world view where I could start a new life and disappear. But before I could begin to wrestle with my long-range life plans, I had to survive the next twenty-four hours. I had to get back to Miami, work fast and leave quickly—within hours—or I'd likely be caught, tortured, killed, and cut up and then dumped in the Everglades where my last actions on this earth would be to be chewed up, gulped down, and shit out by some hungry gator. I could mourn Julie and decide what to do with the rest of my life once I was out of South Florida. Until then, I had no life to plan.

Even though I still had plenty of loose ends, the beginning of a plan was coming together in my head. I opened my eyes. As hard as it was to imagine, I was about to step out into a brand-new world that was even crazier than the last one I'd been living in.

Chapter 8

The security and police presence at Stapleton looked to be typical, which meant the police were slow to put a lockdown on the city. They also likely hadn't yet identified Julie and didn't know she had flown in from Miami yesterday and was planning on leaving today. Even though we bought tickets separately, it meant police wouldn't yet be looking at that manifest and that wasn't a bad thing for me. It allowed me clear passage. I broke my own rules about travelling alone and buying last minute, one-way tickets, changing to catch the first non-stop out of Denver. I was wheels down at Miami International Airport shortly after 1 p.m. My mind had been racing and my body was in motion nearly every minute since stepping out of the shower late yesterday afternoon.

Julie and I had learned to be both self-sufficient and creative in our travels. Rolls of sheet plastic and folded cardboard boxes were always packed—and almost always used to convey the cash away from Denver and back to Miami in a FedEx container.

This trip, the cash had a traveling buddy—ten kilos of

cocaine. Yesterday, I'd wrapped it all securely and had it overnighted to the Villas' South Beach mansion for an early afternoon delivery today. Yeah, as crazy a place as that seemed to be doing business from, it really was the natural choice for this deal—unless Roberto was there waiting for it or came in through the front door while I was unpacking it. I was counting on that not happening. There was no scenario where I survived if Roberto got to Miami before I had a chance to leave.

I'd already made some calls to people I knew in Miami who would take the cocaine off my hands at a cut rate price, no questions asked. That I was doing this in the Villa mansion was ballsy, but it gave the deal the air of legitimacy I needed to pull it off. I'd combine these new funds with the money Julie and I had already stashed in our bank here, convert it all to accounts in another secure bank I could access from anywhere, and get the fuck out of South Florida and never come back. If Roberto was alive—which I had slowly convinced myself that he was—I wasn't going to make it easy for him to find me.

The police in Denver weren't a concern. My name was unknown, and in those days, there was no phalanx of cameras or internet searching to aid authorities in finding me. No, Roberto was my sole concern.

The plan would work as long as I got it all accomplished in the next several hours—which was all I figured I had before Roberto was due to show up. He was a survivor, and I was sure he'd find a way to get out of Denver—it was just a matter of when—and that depended on just how badly hurt he'd been in the shootout and whether or not he could get bandaged up quickly.

Once I came to the conclusion that he was the survivor, I never once doubted he would evade police and begin to hunt me down. I was banking on the belief that he was injured and alone in Denver, and he would need to take care of his injuries and avoid police before attempting to come back home to Miami. That that would take some time. Even so, he'd push himself to move as quickly as possible to increase his chances of finding me. He was a smart man who would be doing his own strategizing. He would realize time was his enemy. He knew I would come to Miami and locating me here was his best and possibly only chance of ever finding me, his money and his drugs. On top of that, he would realize his best alibi was to be alive in Miami when police came knocking to see if he was the lone survivor who had escaped the Denver bloodbath.

I'd live to see another day—only if I could manage to be quick about my work. If I didn't, well, Roberto would get what he wanted, and I'd get that trip to the Everglades in the back of his Land Rover.

Sure, I could have just taken the cash and left the cocaine in that hotel room. With Roberto alive—something I hadn't considered then—that would have been less risky and possibly more likely to assuage Roberto and convince him to allow me to escape with the money and my life. It would have left him something for all his troubles and maybe, just maybe, he wouldn't come after me. But who knew? Did anything I did make a difference more than what I didn't do? Not helping him get out of there alive was likely my most egregious sin in Roberto's view. Add to that my taking the cash and the coke—and being the lone, surviving witness—he needed me dead.

Was I being greedy? Perhaps. But I didn't give a shit. I wanted all the money for MY troubles. Julie was dead, and my world was shattered. Roberto would hunt me like an animal regardless. And besides, the money and additional cash the coke would generate would help guarantee that I would be able to disappear forever.

I drove around the block several times, parking in two separate spaces just to watch the house. Dripping with nervous sweat, I surveilled the South Beach neighborhood thoroughly to make sure the Feds or local cops weren't on to anything—that they weren't lying in wait for me—and more importantly, that Roberto—bandaged and bloody, wasn't waiting inside his house for me, sitting comfortably in an armchair, blunderbuss in hand.

Once assured the house was empty and the coast clear, I broke in—I knew I could find a spare key by the back gate, and I knew how to disable the security system—perks of being a trusted confidante. The package was delivered to the house at two-thirty, and one of our mutual "friends" came by at three o'clock sharp for the coke. He couldn't believe the deal he was getting and as I had hoped, didn't ask a lot of questions, hightailing it outta there as fast as he could.

With that magic trick pulled out of my hat, I tucked an additional $100,000 in my bag, locked up the Villa house, climbed in Julie's car and headed to my local bank. Inside, I met with my favorite assistant manager in a side office and handed him an envelope with $25,000 in it, $15,000 more than our usual arrangement. The cash from the bloody Denver deal plus today's side deal—minus twenty-five grand in loose bills for me to use in my upcoming travels. I laid out my needs: this stash and the money that Julie and I had placed in our safe deposit box was no longer safe and needed to be moved—a tidy sum that now added up to almost 3.2 million dollars. I needed to have access to it from most anywhere on the East Coast. I wanted all that money to gain interest and grow. I needed not to be tied to it in any illegal way and I needed not to be traced back here. And it all had to happen now.

All this he told me he could do, for an additional $25,000. Thankfully, that's how Miami worked in those days. I looked him in the eye and shook his hand. I counted out the twenty-five grand and he went upstairs to make it happen while I sat in my little room off the safe deposit area and wondered what I hadn't thought of that could trip me up, put me in jail, leave me penniless or kill me.

Just before closing time, he came back in with a pile of paperwork for me to sign. My money would be wire transferred to Chase Manhattan. He had set it all up, including arrangements for me to meet a compatriot of his at a Chase bank branch outside Washington D.C., where I would receive my passbooks and checks attached to the new account. He tried to extort an extra $10,000 for his friend up north, but I told him he could take that ten grand out of the $50 large I'd just given him.

"I realize what you're doing here has risk," I interrupted as he pleaded for more. "And for that, I am willing to pay. I handed you twenty-five thousand dollars when I walked in and I laid another twenty-five thousand on top of that. Another ten grand makes me kind of twitchy and angry. You don't want that."

"But…"

"No buts, listen," I said. I spoke in an understated, low but firm and steady voice. I had learned quite a bit from watching the Villas work their transactions. "You've got fifty thousand dollars that you didn't have two hours ago. That, plus the thousands I've already given you for your help and indiscretion. That's all you're getting from me." I stopped for effect. Our eyes were locked.

"I think I've been quite generous. Keep in mind, for the amount I have paid you, I expect perfection. Absolute perfection." I stopped again. Our eyes were still locked. He swallowed hard, knowing from my tone I wasn't finished.

"My accounts will be fully functional. I'll be able to deposit or withdraw as needed from any branch along the East Coast whenever I want. Without suspicion. I also expect that my full amount will be there. Do we understand each other?"

There was a short pause. He finally had the defeated, timid look I had expected him to have by this point in the conversation. But just in case he wasn't fully committed, I decided to press him a little more.

"If any of this is not the case, I'll come back here. I'll find you, torture you in front of your family, kill them while you watch, and then I'll cut you apart piece by piece and feed you to alligators in the Everglades." Yes, the Villa brothers had given me quite an education.

I had maintained unblinking eye contact the entire time. He nodded his head slowly and sadly but said nothing more.

I'd never spoken to anyone like that before but had heard threats like that—had seen threats like that carried out by the Villa brothers—and knew they were very effective.

Without breaking eye contact, I said, "Good. Then our business is concluded."

Our eyes remained locked. He swallowed a big, dry gulp and silently nodded. Ours had been a friendly, win-win relationship. Up until this moment I'd never spoken to him like this, and the shock and realization of what he'd just done, the sort of person I likely was and what I would do to him if this all didn't work out, may have just now fully dawned on him.

I'd been around the Villas long enough to learn how to make people do the things you wanted, the things needed to make these sorts of deals successful.

I pushed the deposit box toward him, stood up, and slung my bag over my shoulder as I headed upstairs and toward the door.

I jumped in Julie's car and drove north up Collins Avenue, through South Beach with the trendy shops, bars, and restaurants to my left—and the Atlantic to my right. I had the windows down and breathed in the fresh sea air. I drank in the sights, telling myself this would be the last time I'd ever be here. I was lucky to be able to experience it this one last time. To come back—ever—was to face the possibility of meeting Roberto, and thus, certain death.

I drove west. I stopped the car about a block from the Miami Auto Depot and decided to ditch it there. Next, I bought a used 1980 Ford Bronco with cash, drove out to I-95, and headed north for parts unknown and a new life.

Chapter 9

The Villa brothers were born to devoutly Catholic parents in Havana, in pre-Castro Cuba. They were four, six and eight when Castro came to power. While not rich by any means before Castro, their family did well enough, and they were comfortable. Their father was a mechanic and their mother worked in one of the city's upscale casinos. But as was the case throughout the country, the Revolution changed everything.

From comfortable to chaotic, well-fed to hungry, reasonably well off to barely getting by, they were eventually forced to give up their home and move to a three room flat above a mostly empty grocery store. Roberto was ten when he and his family left their homeland for the shores of the Promised Land. They had sold all their worldly belongings to risk crossing the Strait of Florida, crammed into a small boat along with two dozen other expatriates with little food and water and no bathroom.

By the time they left Cuba, Roberto had seen too many of the men in his neighborhood—including his father—hauled off for questioning, never to be seen again. He'd seen others rousted from their bed in the middle of the night, dragged out to the street and beaten for all to see and hear. These beatings weren't designed to weed out conspirators, but instead, to instill fear into the masses. Listening to a man being beaten to within an inch of his life in the dead still of the night will leave the most hardened person with a weakened resolve. Hearing him beg for his life with his last words, only to be silenced by a rifle shot to the head, virtually guarantees quiet, sheep-like obedience.

These nighttime lessons taught Roberto at a very young age just how valuable unexpected, violent behavior can help shape results. And while he had not yet struck another person or pointed a gun at anyone, by the time he crawled up out of the water on to a South Florida beach, he was a believer that the timely use of fists and bullets could give a man whatever he wanted.

Life in Miami's Little Havana neighborhood did nothing to change this belief. The organized drug trade there was run with brutal efficiency by a small, well-armed group of Cuban Americans who doled out beatings along with their cocaine, heroin, and pot. And they did more than teach Roberto how it worked from afar; they took him and his brothers in to help run the business. Who better to deliver illegal drugs than underage minors? Addicts and abusers were hesitant to mistreat them or haggle over price and they knew the neighborhood alleys, back doors, and escape routes better than anyone. And they were minors—and therefore, were immune to the fullest extent of the law if they were ever caught by police. In exchange, the boys made enough money to support their mother and the household and learned from the ground up how to run a drug cartel. And part of that was the application of violence to get a job done.

Roberto witnessed dozens of beatings by the time he was twelve. He saw his first torture and execution when he was thirteen, and at fourteen, he pulled the trigger in his first murder. They were becoming so successful, that by the time he was fifteen, he and his brothers were targeted by a rival gang. Juan and Carlos escaped unharmed, but Roberto was shot twice—once in the thigh, and once in the stomach. Wounded, he managed to drag himself to the home of one of his gang's leaders, where a friendly doctor was called in to remove the bullets—without anesthesia. That incident helped cement Roberto's legend. By the time he was twenty-one, he was running the gang that had taught him the ropes—having survived or killed all the group's previous leaders. Three short years later, he struck a deal with other gangs and organizations that consolidated his reach over most of the cocaine trade in South Florida. All he had to do in exchange, was hand over his heroin and pot businesses. He was an early believer in the growth potential of the coke market and wanted to focus his full attention on it. He was shrewd, tactical, and dangerous, and in this business, that made him very successful.

It also made him fearless of men and their threats and of the sorts of things most of us are all afraid of—like getting shot.

When Roberto came to, face down in the hotel room, he knew immediately that while he had been shot and was severely injured, he would not die from his wounds. The pistols the yuppie dealers had been carrying got off a lot of rounds in a short amount of time, but thankfully, none carried the punch and destructive power of his brother's .44 or sawed-off shotgun.

He rolled over and sat up. He had been shot four times—twice in his left shoulder, once in his chest, and once in his right thigh. The blunt force trauma had knocked him out cold, but miraculously, none of the bullets appeared to have nicked any arteries or major organs. And through some quirk of fate, all seemed to have gone straight through him. He'd lost a fair amount of blood—and needed to contain the bleeding—but considering how many holes he had in him, he wasn't bleeding too badly. He was in pain, but he was mobile and alive. And by the looks of it, he might be the only one. There was no movement from the pile of bodies at his feet.

A siren was wailing from somewhere down the hall. He heard police and ambulance sirens in the distance, getting closer. He needed to check on his brothers—hopefully they were also just hurt and not dead—patch himself and them up the best he could in a hurry, grab the cash and cocaine and get the fuck out of here before the police stormed this place. This was not the outcome he wanted, but he'd been in worse fixes. The death of the yuppie dealers was his main goal and would give him the clear shot he wanted to gain control of the Colorado coke trade. And in doing so, he would quadruple his profits.

He slowly stood up—standing too quickly could cause him to pass out—he had no desire to be found by the police in this room and be jailed in this cold, foreign state. He stumbled a few steps into the bathroom, flipped on the light, and gave himself a quick once over. He looked like he'd been working in a slaughterhouse. He was covered in blood, and his clothes were tattered. He'd have to add cleaning up and finding a change of clothes to the list of things he needed to do fast in order to get out of here alive.

Back in the room's hallway, it took just seconds to realize both Juan and Carlos were dead. They lay side by side, as if they were napping in a faux peaceful scene that belied the violence that had taken place here just moments before. One of Juan's arms had been blown clear off. They had rushed in to the room first and had been in front of him. Both had taken many more gunshots than he had. It was a lot to take in and he was numb from what he saw, but knew it was better to contain the emotion now—it would wash over him later. This numbness would be replaced by sadness, grief and finally anger—which would require action and perhaps revenge to be taken out on any surviving members of Chris's yuppie posse.

But all who laid here before him—like his brothers— were obviously dead. Bullet-ridden, pieces of their bodies were plastered on the walls of the confined hallway space. Julie was lovely and desirable no more, having taken a slug from Juan's .44 to the head. It was too bad she and Dan had to be here for this, but he'd decided it was the best place for an ambush and ultimately, they were expendable. He'd always liked them. They were calm, fun, and honest in their dealings.

Except today, thought Roberto, as he gazed around the room, looking for duffel bags and Dan's body.

Chris and his hired guns had opened fire instantaneously as if they were expecting trouble. As if Dan and Julie had tipped them off the moment the hotel room door closed behind them. How else could they have been ready? How else could they have gotten off so many shots so quickly, and killed so efficiently when surprised? They couldn't have, Roberto surmised, unless there was no surprise.

As he formed these thoughts, he stared at the pile of bodies clumped together in a warlike relief.

Dan was not in the pile. Not among the dead. Not in the room.

How was that possible? He'd seen them both walk in with the yuppies. Dan should have been directly in the line of fire.

Unless he warned the yuppies and dove for cover as the door burst open, leaving his allies and girlfriend to suffer the brunt of the attack.

Roberto stepped through the bodies and looked around the room. The money bag Chris had been carrying was bloody, discarded, and empty.

Slowly working his way around the room, he began picking through belongings that were spread out on the floor; a bag that was obviously Julie's, a pile of men's clothes—likely Dan's—he looked under the bed, walked back through the bodies and looked in the closet and bathroom.

Not only was Dan not here, but neither was his luggage bag. Nor the money. Nor the coke.

Roberto was no longer numb. He'd skipped sadness and grief and gone straight to anger. Red hot, murderous anger.

Dan.

He had avoided being killed and had managed to escape. He had betrayed him and his brothers. Dan hadn't even checked to see if he was alive, and he didn't just run for his life, he'd made off with the cash and coke. Roberto's cash and coke.

"I will take back what is ours and avenge you," Roberto said out loud, in a low, seething spew, as a promise to his dead brothers.

This carnage was avoidable. He'd had a good, clean plan, thought Roberto. Once he settled things with Dan, and mourned his brother, he'd get back to the business of taking over the lucrative Colorado cocaine business.

The sirens stopped ringing, bringing him momentarily out of his rage and thoughts of the future. He had to move fast.

Roberto reached down and grabbed the pile of Dan's clothes that remained and walked back to the bathroom. He stripped down, turned on the shower and stepped in to wash away the blood that covered him, getting a quick look at his wounds while he did. The water hurt like hell but cleaned him up, and he was pretty sure he'd live.

He stepped out, dried off, and began putting on clothes. He found some packing tape and used that as he secured wash cloths and small hand towels against the bullet holes in his body and then put layers of shirts on over them, using all of Dan's remaining shirts and a loose-fitting jacket. He put on a pair of shorts, packed in some more wash cloths and pulled on loose khakis to hide his leg wound. He would need to concentrate to avoid walking with a limp until he was far away from cops and flashing lights.

The cover—which took all of four minutes to accomplish—was enough to hide his wounds and keep the blood from seeping through, at least for a few minutes—which was all he hoped he needed to escape. He grabbed his wallet and walked back out to the room's hallway where he took both Juan's and Carlos's wallets, then tucked Juan's .44 and one of the yuppies' handguns into his waistband and walked out into the quiet hallway.

Chapter 10

Roberto walked as quickly as he could down the hotel hallway, listening for noises behind the doors. Even though the sirens had stopped, the ringing in his ears made it hard to hear anything. Regardless, this floor appeared to be deserted. If there had been other people staying here, the gun battle had cleared them out.

He found a stairwell, and once he opened the door to enter, he could easily hear people down below him noisily making their way to the lobby. He needed to join them. The fleeing crowd would give him cover. He kept walking down, feeling pain with each step he took. Once he reached the second floor, he stopped and waited for others who were still coming out of the top floors to catch up with him. He didn't want to emerge into the lobby alone.

Two thirty-something Latino ladies were closing in on him. They looked like they'd seen a ghost. He faced them and asked, "What is going on up there?" He hoped his English was clear enough.

"We heard gunshots. A *lot* of gunshots," said one of them.

"Like a war. There must have been hundreds of shots. I thought people were going to burst through our door and kill us," added the other. They looked like sisters.

The first one, probably the big sister, chimed back in. She said, "We called the lobby, they said to stay put, but I say to hell with that. We're getting out of here! So we grabbed what we could and ran like hell."

As they came down to the landing Roberto was standing on, he said, "Yeah, that's what they told me too, but I'm with you. I say we get out of here fast!" He decided to cover his tracks. "By the way, I'm Juan," he lied.

"Hey," said the older of the two, "I'm Eva, and this is my sister, Cecilia."

Acting as normally as he could under the circumstances, he reached for the small bags they each had slung over their shoulders. "Nice to meet you. Let me get those," he said. It was more of a gentlemanly movement and statement than a question, and he delivered it with a reassuring smile as he reached out, hoping his actions and their Latin bond would evaporate any mistrust.

"Aw, thanks," they both said, almost in unison as they handed the bags over.

He had done all he could do to maintain a smile and not show that the added weight of the bags sent waves of pain shooting through him. Blood hadn't yet soaked through his clothes, but it was just a matter of time until it did. He needed to get out of here quickly.

"No problem let's *all* get the hell out of here!" he said, with just the right amount of bravado. The three of them walked down the rest of the stairs and out into the lobby together.

The lobby was swarming with SWAT members, regular cops, firefighters and paramedics. "Holy shit, Eva," said the younger sister. "We got to get some pics of this! Ma's never going to believe it!"

SWAT looked poised to head up the same stairwell the three of them had just come down. Five fully armed, locked and loaded, paramilitary cops stood at the ready, rifles poised and pointed right at them as they stepped into the lobby.

"Folks, what floors were you on. Did you see or hear anything?" questioned one of the cop commandos holding a semi-automatic rifle in front of him.

"I was on three," said Roberto without hesitation.

"Six," said the sisters at the same time.

Looking at the sisters, the cop continued. He asked, "Did you see or hear anything?"

"Just the alarms," said Roberto, again, getting in fast with his answer.

"Jesus H. Christ," said Eva. "There was a freakin' war going on above us on seven. There must have been hundreds of shots in like, ten seconds, and then, nothing."

"Yeah, we called down to the front desk," Cecilia said. "They must have been swamped, I could hear phones ringing in the background. But the guy just said to stay put and hung up. We stuck around for about ten minutes and then got the hell outta there though."

"Are any of you injured?"

"No," all three exclaimed at once.

"OK, folks, make your way through the lobby and check in with our people in the parking lot. You're safe now."

That depended on Roberto. Who was getting antsy talking to the commando with two guns tucked in his pants and blood beginning to seep through all four of his wounds. He grabbed the girls gently by the elbows and pointed them toward the front door. Being with them and not alone gave the outward signal that they were together and not part of some running gun battle.

"Let's head out and put these bags in your car so you don't lose them in all this chaos," Roberto said.

He'd passed the first wave of police scrutiny, but he needed to completely clear this scene before he felt the least bit secure.

"You're so thoughtful Juan, thanks!" said Cecilia.

Roberto maneuvered everyone through the parking lot, telling the cops and paramedics who came up to them that they were just putting their bags in their car and that they'd be back.

Once at their car, a late model Honda, he quietly pulled Carlos's big .44 from his waistband and held it close.

"Jesus Christ on a popsicle stick," said a wide-eyed Eva. Her younger sister said nothing, despite her mouth being wide open.

"Girls, I don't want any trouble and I sure don't want to have to hurt you, but I need to leave now. Just stay calm and quiet and get in the car. We're going to take a short ride and then this will all be over."

Roberto had to get to the small executive airport on the

other side of Stapleton, where his chartered jet and ride home to Miami waited. He was sure he was only minutes behind Dan and was guessing that if Dan wasn't too badly injured, he'd convert his return ticket to Miami to the first available non-stop, get his savings and belongings, and leave town as quickly as he could. Even if he couldn't get there before him, he could get home and patched up and put a plan in motion to find Dan, his cash and his coke. Swift revenge would be his.

The sisters clutched each other and immediately began trembling and whimpering.

"Son of a bitching bastard," Eva said under her breath.

"Girls, now just behave. Who has the keys?"

"I do," said Eva. "But…"

"No buts Eva, just unlock the car, you're going to drive, and Cecilia is going to get in the back seat with the bags. I'll ride in front with you. We're going to take a short, ten-minute ride, and then we're done. OK? That's it. Ten minutes."

Cecelia got in the back seat obediently. Reluctantly, Eva got behind the wheel and Roberto got in next to her, leveling the gun at her.

"I know you're thinking you need to do something to get us noticed, maybe gunning this car into some other cars, beeping the horn the whole way, making as much noise as you can so all these cops here will come to your rescue," he said, and he simply paused and stared into her eyes, unblinking for a few seconds. "And that's a pretty good thought, Eva," he finally said, with a calm nod of his head.

"They will hear all the racket, see the commotion and

come, yes. But it will be too late. I'll have shot you and your sister dead by then with this big, awful gun. If you make a move I don't like, I'll spray your brains all over the inside of this car, turn around and blow your sister's head clean off. I'll probably get caught and shot and not make it out alive either, but I've already come to grips with the possibility I may die today."

Roberto paused, then, staring her straight in the eyes, continued. "The question is, have you?" he asked.

They eyeballed each other silently. Cecilia was whimpering loudly in the back seat. She'd been considering that plan exactly.

"I'd rather not die," Eva said in a whisper.

"I didn't think so. Let's get outta here nice and slow," Roberto said, as he motioned with his gun.

Eva took a deep breath, held it for a moment and exhaled, then started the car and looked over at Roberto. Before putting it in gear she said, "You're going to die from those gunshot wounds anyway."

"What makes you think I've been shot or that I'm dying? Just because you heard a bunch of gunshots and now, I'm holding this gun on you, you think I'm wounded and dying? You some sort of clairvoyant?" He let out a snort of laughter.

"I'm a doctor. And you're bleeding through your clothes in two spots, one in your chest, and the other by your abdomen or crotch. I'd say you'll be dead inside of five hours unless you get medical help immediately." Eva didn't make eye contact while she spoke.

The inside of the car got quiet instantly. Cecilia stopped

whimpering. Both sisters stared at Roberto. The gun was still trained on Eva as Roberto slowly turned his head to look forward out the window at nothing in particular. Pursing his lips, it was his turn to take a long, full thoughtful breath and exhale it slowly and loudly. He could feel the life draining from him and had begun to consider that getting on a plane without first getting patched up may not be his smartest play.

After what seemed like an eternity to the sisters, he turned back at Eva. "I've been shot four times, doctor. Not twice. And I need you to get me to my plane, so I can get out of here and get medical attention. I'll be good as gold and all patched up in six hours."

"You'll be dead in four. Five tops," Eva said. Again, she didn't look at him while she spoke.

Cecelia yelled from the back seat, "Eva, shut up and quit arguing. Just drive him where he wants to go and let him do whatever he wants so we can get out of this alive."

"No honey. If we drive him to the airport, he'll just kill us there. I've got a better idea." Eva looked over at Cecelia, then Roberto.

This was a smart one, Roberto thought. She knew what sort of person he was just by looking him in the eye. He was beginning to believe she was right about how much time he had, too. He might even have less. He could feel the coldness beginning to set in. He was bleeding out. It was just a matter of time before he faded into unconsciousness. In that light, killing them seemed like a waste. He needed to use them.

"So, what's your idea?" he asked softly.

"You put that gun down. Look me in the eye and shake my hand and promise me you will not harm either of us," Eva said. She paused, took a deep breath, and then continued speaking. "I'll take you to my house. It's less than an hour away. I've got a pretty full medical kit there. As long as no major organs have been hit, I can sew you up and stop all that bleeding. It'll take me a few hours. Then you take my car and leave. Go wherever it is you came from. Leave us. That's it. No cops. We live. You live."

Roberto liked this Eva. She was calm under pressure and ballsy. He had to decide whether or not to put his life in her hands.

"If you live so close, why are you staying at an airport hotel?" Roberto asked. He believed no one and was suspicious that she might be planning on waiting for him to pass out as they drove and then dump him or take him to the police.

"We were flying out later for a vacation trip to South America."

"Where?"

"Peru."

"Nice. A very beautiful place." Roberto could feel himself getting tired. He had to make a decision, soon.

He paused again and thought it over. She was no drug dealer who lied for a living. She was a doctor, steeped in morals. She was telling the truth. She would do this for him if he gave her his word. She would trust him.

"No anesthesia. You sew me up and make sure I'm going to make it. No phone calls. No cops. No bullshit. We all get back in the Honda afterward and drive back to my plane. No phone calls. I have fifty thousand dollars in cash with me. When we get to my plane, and there are no cops there preventing my departure, I'll give you the cash—all fifty thousand of it—for taking care of me, the use of your car and your time. Then you two can take that vacation in style."

"I don't want your money. You don't have to do that," Eva said.

"Yes, I do. Fifty grand and my word I will never harm either of you. You fix me up and keep it between us, forever. That's the deal. Take it or leave it."

Eva turned, looked out the front window and then in the rearview mirror at Cecelia, who was trembling again and holding in a whimper.

Eva started the car. "We'll take it," she said.

Chapter 11

Eva had never seen a man capable of withstanding this kind of pain without anesthesia of any sort. With barely a grimace on his face, he gave his instructions in a calm, controlled voice.

"Dig out any bullets or pieces of bullets and any loose bone fragments. Repair any damage the best you can and sew me up," he said. "I need to leave here as quickly as possible. I seek vengeance."

For a man lying on his back on a kitchen table in a stranger's house, having surgery performed on him by a doctor he just met—while he was wide awake—this man was extremely calm. And focused. She pitied whomever it was he was aiming to find.

"Vengeance." Roberto mouthed the words at least a dozen times while she worked. It seemed to put him in to some sort of meditative trance that took his mind off the pain.

Where that vengeance would be and against whom was of no concern to her. She had learned at a young age that you couldn't stop a man like this from harming or killing, you could only stay out of his way. And getting clear of him was her main goal now.

She was relieved and amazed to see that only one of the bullets, the one in his leg, remained lodged in him. No arteries or organs or bones were struck or damaged. This calculating man was a lucky one. It took her just over three hours to repair him and sew him up. She made him sit still for a bit after the triage and drink orange juice. While he'd lost a lot of blood and would be weak and sore for a while, these wounds would not kill him. He used her phone, and in his native tongue, told the man on the other end—a pilot from the sounds of things—to get some rest and that they would likely leave first thing in the morning.

Roberto hung up the phone and looked at the sisters. Staring at Eva, he said, "You have steady hands and do nice work. Thank you."

Eva said nothing. The three of them were sitting around Eva's kitchen table. The sisters had cleaned the room after the makeshift surgery. Roberto was still slowly sipping orange juice. Again, he spoke to Eva.

"I am not ready to leave you yet. I need to be still for a while longer and my pilot wants to wait until morning to leave. While I'm sure we would all rather not wait that long, we will all sit here in this room and rest until then."

He looked at them both, expecting them to say something.

"I apologize, but I will need to tie each of you up until then. I cannot afford that either of you do something hasty and foolish while we wait. We are so close to ending this thing without any further violence, I would hate for something unfortunate to occur."

"You don't need to tie us up," Cecilia said in a fearful, almost tearful voice. "We have done everything you have asked of us."

"True. You have. But I am a man who takes no chances. In the morning, I will untie you and you will drive me to the executive airport next to Stapleton. If all is well there and I am able to leave without incident, I will give you the fifty grand in cash, your car, and both of your lives back. You have my word on that."

He paused a moment. His gaze was now expressionless, cold, riveting.

"However, if you do not remain calm and quiet here and you break free and perhaps call the police, or there is the least bit of trouble at the airport, or the slightest suspicion that places me in danger when I am there, I will kill you both."

The room was silent. He slowly turned his icy stare to Eva. Their eyes were locked.

"I will kill you," he repeated the words slowly, pausing between each. There was no doubt in this room that he would do this. Eva remained motionless. Cecelia was trembling.

After what seemed like five minutes but was probably more like thirty seconds, he inhaled deeply and smiled, his outward demeanor doing a full 180.

"But none of us want that to happen, so why should it?" he asked, smiling broadly, placing both his hands palms down on the table to make his point. The .44 lay between them.

"You want me to leave and never come back, as do I,"

Roberto said. "You have kept your end of our agreement, and I will honor mine. I only want to return to my home. I have a debt to repay there. There is someone else I care more about than you. Much more. A man who has betrayed me, stolen from me and caused me great pain. I live now so that I can find this man, no matter where he is or how long it takes me to find him. I live so that I can look him in the eye as I take his life from him."

Part 2

Chapter 12

As one of my favorite tattered t-shirts proclaimed for all to see, Life is Good. Looking out over the vast Atlantic Ocean 35,000 feet below, making our way back to our luxurious suburban home outside Pittsburgh after two weeks in Europe with my beautiful loving wife and kids, it was hard to argue the point.

Growing up in a modest, one car, middle class family environment, I had never imagined I would be rich enough to afford such a trip, let alone several trips like this a year. After escaping Colorado alive, I never thought I'd be lucky enough to live this long, find love again, and build a life like this.

But here I was, thirty years after that violent day that ripped my life apart, with riches beyond my wildest dreams and a life that appeared to all who looked in on it to be postcard picture perfect. Trips like this were the norm, not the exception. And even though I didn't lead an ostentatious life, I lacked for nothing. We lived an upper middle-class existence but had the financial assets of those living in the top one-percent.

Money was not a concern. I'd taken my illicit millions and invested them wisely—and had been lucky enough to have caught the wave on stocks like AOL, Apple, Google, and more—doubling, quadrupling, and quadrupling again what I'd started with.

Driving north from Florida thirty plus years ago, my focus was on surviving that day, and then the next, and the next. It wasn't until years later that I felt I had put enough distance between myself and Roberto—that I'd left no crumbs along the way for him to find—and that my trail, and not me, was cold and dead.

I had fled north to Upstate New York, a place where I grew up as a boy and felt comfortable. A place where I knew the people and how they behaved, as well as out of the way places where no one but a local could find me—and then, only with some doing.

I stopped at Army-Navy stores along the drive north from Florida and put together an acceptable cache of camping equipment—backpack, tent, sleeping bag, fishing rod and tackle, cooking utensils, boots, clothes and such. I also accumulated a variety of non-perishable food supplies.

I drove through my hometown of Utica but didn't stop—that would have made it too easy for Roberto, and one of the first places he would likely send his soldiers to search for me. Instead, I continued north and into the edge of the Adirondack Park, a vast, mountainous, lake-filled six-million-acre void that had been a hiking and camping playground for me as a young boy. I knew large swatches of it well, and knew that for someone who didn't, finding me would be virtually impossible.

I turned off route 12 near Forestport, shopped for enough canned and dried food to fill my car—which I would use as a grocery store in the woods—then headed east along a sketchy road that eventually turned to dirt, skirted around North Lake and came to an end at a trailhead to South Lake. I was now twenty miles from where I'd turned off route 12. I left a note on my dashboard that the occupant was camping and kayaking the nearby Black River and would return in a month. Once the note was in place, I filled my backpack with food, gear, and guns, and headed in the opposite direction, hauling everything through scrub brush around the lake until I found the lean-to, a place I'd remembered from boyhood hikes. Except for snakes and raccoons, it looked like it hadn't had a tenant in years.

That spot was about as far off the grid as I could get and still feel in control. I cleared it out, made myself at home, and fished and hunted for small game. I ate up my supplies and spent what remained of the summer exploring miles of the densely wooded area that I hoped would offer me solace and protection. In my early hikes through the rugged, rolling hills, marshes, river and lakefront, I discovered a small, older cabin far on the other side of South Lake with well water, no electricity, virtually no access and a good 360-degree line of sight. I eventually found the owner, who was willing to be overpaid for it—moved in before winter hit hard—and spent my days and nights there, a virtual recluse from the world for the next two years.

I was probably one of fewer than a hundred people who

lived within a thirty-mile radius year-round. I kayaked, cut wood, fished, hunted in the warm seasons and snowmobiled and cross country skied in the winter—in short, I acted like I belonged. I kept loaded shotguns tucked away in every room in the house—a .357 Magnum under my pillow, and a small handgun and a hunting knife on my person at all times—even in the outhouse, where I also had a loaded shotgun tucked under a loose floor board.

I lived there, as a virtual recluse, except for an ever-vigilant German shepherd puppy I raised and named Jules, hoping that time and isolation would guarantee me safety and eventually, a routine to normalcy—whatever that was. There was no bump in the night, no growl followed by an explosion, no assassin crawling through the woods, no knife slipped between my ribs as I hiked or walked, and no bullet to the head while I slept. No one found me and even though I eventually began to wonder if anyone was searching, I stayed put.

I repaired a rowboat, bought a canoe and added some minor conveniences to my encampment so that I could survive what was a snowy, icy, cold, and lonely existence for five months out of the year.

On my warm weather monthly visits to town for supplies, I'd stock up on books and magazines—a mish-mash of current events and fiction—and I began studying accounting and business as well as architecture and building techniques. It came in handy. I used the knowledge to track and grow my finances, and to slowly reconstruct my former warm weather camp into a year-round home. I also started a correspondence course with the relatively nearby Syracuse University, and eventually decided to re-join the world there as a student of architecture.

As rejuvenating and grounding as my experience in the backwoods was, the life of a recluse was not intended for this 20-year-old. I needed to be around people, needed human interaction, and yeah, to get laid every now and again. I needed to get out in the world and to figure out what kind of life I could have before it just passed me by while I wallowed in the past, afraid of dangers I couldn't see.

I put Julie and my past to rest as best I could. I cried myself to sleep, realizing the mistakes I made ruined my life and took hers. And I figured that while Roberto might truly never give up his hope of finding me and getting his hands around both my neck and his money, he had likely set his death quest aside for the time being to more fully re-join his old world and generate some new cash. Being a drug kingpin in Miami had its perks—and its dangers. Coming back from Colorado all shot up and alone might present an opening to competition. While I was hopeful one of those up-and-comers would knock Roberto off, I wasn't betting on it. If my past experience and his history were any indicator, Roberto would show neither mercy nor weakness. If anyone dared to step into his realm to try and seize his throne, they would be obliterated.

Regardless, as long as he lived, he would never forget me. Not ever.

Even though I hadn't shot him or his brothers. Even though I was a victim of the circumstances that he set in motion. Even though he would have taken—just as I had taken—the drugs and cash, he would not forget, and he could not forgive.

No. The Roberto I had come to know would not only never forget, but in fact he would also blame me for taking both his cash and cocaine. He would eventually somehow begin to believe that I was actually to blame for the shootout and the deaths of his brothers. He would work it and manipulate it until I became the reason for every misfortune that happened and for every missed opportunity that came afterward.

This was the reason I hid in the mountains for two years and then decided to disappear for another four years; hiding in plain sight at Syracuse University.

I put some of my money to good use there, paying for my tuition and expenses at school, as well as a house with an aggressive security system. I took up martial arts and kept in top shape. I was less of a party animal than most college kids—definitely always passing on Spring Break opportunities in Florida—and concentrated on learning how best to invest my money without drawing suspicion. I focused on learning how to create a career that would allow me a life that could again be rich, in every sense of the word, while keeping me out of the spotlight.

I kept my backwoods hideout—just in case—upgrading the security system and making it a safe, secluded haven, and put my education to good use. I consistently grew my nest egg into a sizeable fortune and managed my career, taking steps from company to company, eventually landing in

Pittsburgh, where I became a partner in a small architectural firm that primarily handled bridge and tunnel projects. Not sexy enough to be noticed but lucrative enough to allow for a comfortably plush life.

I never sp0ke about, nor did I forget about Julie, but I moved on, keeping that part of my life private and locked away from everyone around me. Including my wife.

What purpose would it serve to tell her that my first true love was murdered before my eyes in a shootout? That I was a carefree and reckless drug mule who made millions—and in fact, stole nearly a cool million from one of the biggest drug cartels in the States—which more than likely still had a death sentence on my head. Oh, and the real reason I hate Florida and never want to go there is because I'm still afraid someone there might recognize me and end my life—all our lives. This part of me was something that lived only inside of me.

I looked at Diane stretched out next to me, comfortably still sleeping through the long flight to JFK. Physically, she could have been Julie's sister. Beautiful, voluptuous, and giving, my friends all envied me and stole sideway glances at her whenever they thought it was safe. Emotionally and spiritually, the two were very different but somehow, both had gained my trust and my heart and become one with me. Julie because of the thrills, excitement, adrenaline, and crazy bond we developed in a short, white-hot summer relationship. Diane, because of a yearlong friendship that blossomed happily, and she became my dependable rock, lover, and nurturer of our family.

We met after college in Syracuse, where we were both working at a small construction company—me as an architect, she as the payroll accountant. We've shared many good times and luckily, just a few bad ones over the years. Our two boys, 16 and 18, were about to start their own lives, going to college and setting off in the world on their own courses.

It was too late to tell her about my secret past now. I'd made that choice and decided to live with it. Too many years, experiences, and memories had been lived without it being a part of us. It wouldn't just be something bad that I'd done and wanted to forget, it would be a massive lie of omission that I hadn't told my best friend and soul mate. The time to come clean was past. This part of me had to remain where it was, tucked deep inside, never to come out into the light. To bring it out, to unravel it now, could unravel everything I had built since then. The last thing I wanted was to have to start over. Again.

Chapter 13

We had a few hours to kill in JFK while we waited for our connecting flight to Pittsburgh. Not having a direct route home from London was a nuisance, but hey, we were back amongst the comforts of the good ole' USA and making the best use of the time.

Chris and Dave were at a Starbucks, happily drinking frappes, plugging into the free Wi-Fi and reconnecting with their friends on Facebook. It had been almost a day since they had internet access and god only knows how they had survived.

Diane was strolling from shop to shop, picking up little odds and ends for friends and family, and I was rifling through magazines at a bookstore. The Runner's World I'd bought in London was apparently a British version of the magazine—who would have guessed? Pounds were stones, temperatures were in Celsius and there were just enough other odd British phrases and expressions that I was now considering buying the American version of the magazine, so I could more easily decipher how to become a better runner.

From two stores away across the hallway, I looked up and saw Diane coming toward me casually. She looked as beautiful as ever. You would never guess she'd just come off a restless trans-Atlantic flight. Her blonde hair bounced lightly on her shoulders, framing her face. Her blue eyes shined as she flashed me a smile as our eyes met. She had a couple small bags in hand—always the thoughtful one, she was. I smiled back and was about to lift my hand and give a gentle wave when the voice, close enough to my ear that I felt the hot breath on my neck, hit me like a tidal wave.

"What chew doing, mang?"

The physical jolt was electric, instantly sending a bone chilling wave of nausea through me.

Neither loud nor soft, it was as if the voice came from inside my own head. Not heard in decades except in nightmares, it was instantly recognizable. The words careened through my stunned mind like boulders off canyon walls.

Roberto.

I fully expected the greeting to be followed by the sensation of cold steel slicing through my back, ending my days on earth here in this airline terminal as my wife looked on, horrified. He had finally found me, and I was a dead man. That was that. But, when after a few seconds there was no mortal reprisal dealt to me, I turned slowly where I stood, coming face to face with the man I'd spent years fearing and avoiding.

Game over.

Roberto looked down quickly at the magazine in my hand and then back up, re-establishing a laser lock, eye-to-eye gaze. "You some sort of runner now?"

"Reading about how to stay one step ahead of folks breathing down your neck, trailing you?" His English was perfect. The fake accent, used only as a stage prop, was gone. The smile, as effective as a guillotine, was still there.

But there was something odd about his demeanor. Sarcastic and sublimely violent in his tone, the cocky self-assuredness I'd come to expect from Roberto that summer years ago was missing. Maybe he hadn't "found" me. Maybe he was as shocked and surprised to see me as I was to see him. If he'd been stalking me, wouldn't I now be face down in a pool of my own blood?

After thirty years, could we literally have bumped into each other in the middle of the terminal at JFK, by accident?

He broke eye contact and looked over my shoulder, then looked back at me and now smiling, blurted loudly and excitedly, "How have you been, man? Oh my god, what's it been, like thirty years? Dan-O! I can't believe we ran into each other out of the blue, here, after all these years! Unbelievable! Just bumping into each other and remembering each other, after all that time, like it was yesterday!"

His acting was Oscar worthy.

I was speechless. And helpless. Frozen in place, as if in cement, I was unable to escape the freight train of emotion that was sweeping through my mind and body. Not only was I standing next to the one man in the world who wanted me dead and had the means to do it with a snap of his fingers, he also appeared to be some sort of schizoid with a split personality. What the fuck?

"Don't tell me this is the Mrs.?" Roberto asked, as Diane continued to walk closer.

Not a schizoid. This one is crazy like a fox. Always had been.

"Well Dan, ain't this something?"

It sure was.

The man who wants me dead, was about to meet the woman who pledged me "till death us do part."

And up to a minute ago, neither knew the other existed.

Diane had closed the gap and was standing behind me. She and Roberto were looking past me, at each other, smiling and waiting for introductions.

After a few awkward seconds, I gathered myself as best I could.

"Diane, this is Roberto. Roberto, Diane." I spoke in a low, flat monotone voice, as if something inside me fought to bring these words to life.

Diane stuck her hand out, but Roberto swooped in, brushed by it and gave her the same hug I'd seen him give Julie countless times.

"I always knew your husband was a smart man, and you, my dear, are proof of his brilliance," he said loud enough for anyone nearby to hear. "And lucky."

"Aw, why thank you, Roberto. So, how do you two know each other?" Diane asked, looking back and forth between Roberto and me, waiting to see who would answer.

Before I could think of an answer that made any sense, regardless of its honesty, Roberto spoke first.

"What? I can't believe my name has never come up! Dan,

shame on you." He said it with an overblown sense of disbelief, his one arm still around my wife, the other waving upward dramatically.

"Why, we were friends for the briefest of times, many summers ago, Diane. But we were close. So very close. Like blood brothers really," he said, still smiling broadly. He followed up with a wink in my direction.

"Really?" Diane was turning her head from Roberto, to me, and then back again, eagerly waiting for further explanation about this mystery man whom she had never before heard mentioned. Her quizzical gaze ended on me.

"Miami," the word came out like a croak, from deep within me, forced out by fear.

"Miami," I repeated, clearing my throat as I said it in a more normal voice.

"Thirty years ago. Remember, I've told you about my summer there knocking around before I decided what to do with my life? Before school. Before us." I tried to be as nonchalant as possible, not giving off the slightest sense of the near heart-stopping fear that had built inside me and was choking the life out of me.

"Oh yeah, sure. But you said it wasn't a great time. That you couldn't wait to get back up north. You said you never connected there and really never wanted to go back. I can't believe you had such a close friend there and never told me about him!"

She turned from me to Roberto, and then back at me, smiling. This was quintessential Diane—all smiles, playful, fun, and open. Hey, we were stuck at the airport with a little time on our hands and a new adventure was presented to us. A blast from the past that she could talk with and listen to for colorful stories from the good old days. She was going to make the most of it. Under normal circumstances, it was the kind of behavior I adored. But today, now, I feared it.

"I can't believe that either!" said Roberto, smirking incredulously, winking at me again.

"We should get some coffee and catch up, unless you're in a hurry?" she asked, looking at Roberto.

"Not at all," said Roberto.

"No!" I shouted, before I could stop myself.

They both turned to me.

"I mean, we have to round up the boys and get to our gate and get home. We only have a little time, really," I offered lamely.

"Where is home, Dan?" He peered at me. This was more than a mild curiosity. This was the answer to a decade's long search.

"Pittsburgh," answered Diane. Filling the awkward pause as I stared silently at Roberto—our eyes locked—unable to mouth the word he had so desperately wanted to hear spoken.

He smiled broadly now.

"And boys? You have sons? How wonderful!"

I smiled weakly. Diane kept the conversation going politely, not understanding that with each question answered, the danger to our lives increased exponentially. Roberto was skillfully gathering information.

"Yes, two handsome, smart young men. They're over

there in Starbucks catching up with the world on their phones," she smiled, nodding in their direction.

"We're so very fortunate," Diane continued. "Chris is sixteen and Dave is eighteen. Dave is going to Carnegie Mellon this fall, studying computers. We're so proud."

"As you should be. Such a good university. Ah, teenage boys can be so enjoyable." Roberto turned to me. "And so unpredictable."

"God has truly smiled down on you Dan." Roberto had finally let go of his grip on Diane and was now inching closer to me. He was saying nice things, but the words underscored a more sinister design. He'd always been the master of the double entendre.

"The years have been good to you. And no worries Diane, I understand if you're in a hurry to get home. But we must trade emails and numbers and such. I just—so very recently—decided to come to Pittsburgh on important business and we must get together while I'm there." He looked only at me as he said it, impressing his intent on me so that I had a full appreciation for the underlying message to what he was saying.

"We have so much to catch up on," he added.

"Oh good!" Diane responded with genuine glee.

"Yes, good. It's all good, Diane."

"We should all get together when you visit. It'll bring back old memories for you two and I can hear all the stories."

"Yes, it will," Roberto said. Turning to her quickly, he added, "So, Diane, did you keep your maiden name like a modern working woman, or did you take Dan's?" It was an odd question, but he said it so quickly, so matter-of-factly, that Diane jumped back with an answer just as fast.

"Oh, I'm a Griffin now!" she said quickly, waving her wedding ring proudly.

Roberto smiled at her and then turned back to me. He had what he needed to finally end this after all these years. Not knowing my true last name—and identity—had been his biggest stumbling block.

"Here's to the Griffins of Pittsburgh! Dan, Diane, Chris, and Dave," he said with an exaggerated wave of his hand, like a toast.

Roberto raised an invisible glass; his friendly smile belied his hidden agenda, which could now finally be completed. By a stroke of luck, the man he'd only believed in his dreams that he would someday find, literally bumped into him. And his wife, clearly clueless as to the danger he presented, had given him all the answers he needed to bring his vengeance to their door. Retribution was a Google search away.

"You two finish catching up and trade emails and numbers, I'm going to round up the boys and head to our gate," Diane said, sticking her hand back out for Roberto to shake.

Ever the gentleman with the ladies, he again brushed it aside and closed in for a more intimate goodbye hug.

"Ah Diane, meeting you like this, after so many years, has been like a dream fulfilled for me. I promise you, I will visit you all soon in Pittsburgh."

The words were friendly and whispered through wisps of Diane's hair into her ear. He kissed her gently on the cheek and stepped back.

"You are something else, Roberto."

"Yes, indeed I am."

She pulled back, blew me a kiss, and as she turned to walk away, waved over her shoulder.

Roberto and I were left standing there in the bookstore. Just the two of us, our past, present, and future, exposed and vulnerable. The sound of the Runner's World hitting the floor after slipping through my fingers snapped me back to attention, reaffirming this was present, reality.

"She knows nothing, does she Dan?"

I was silent. The smiles were gone now. We were a mere foot apart. I looked him over from head to toe before answering. Clean shaven, he was dressed impeccably in black slacks, a black blazer over a white collared shirt, and completed the look with expensive Italian leather slip on shoes. His hair, still thick, had a gentlemanly salt and pepper color to it. Roberto looked like a wealthy, proper businessman. In my mind's eye, he had always carried himself like royalty, and the years had done nothing to change that picture.

"You never told her about us. About what you did that summer. You're just a regular, law-abiding guy in her eyes, aren't you?"

I had no words.

"A loving husband and doting father. With a thick bank account, no? But you've been keeping secrets, Dan. Such a naughty boy." He squared off as he said the last few words, now standing directly in front of me.

"What do you want, Roberto? Have you really been searching for me all these years, just so you can break my balls and cause me grief in my marriage? What could you possibly want from me now? Our relationship is over. You killed it, remember?"

My words were dripping with sarcasm and anger, but they fell far short of their mark. I was trying to show him I hadn't given him a thought after the shootout in Denver and had gone my way honestly believing the cord between us was cut clean. He wasn't buying it.

"No, no, no, Dan. We're not all good here. The past is not just the past. I've carried it with me. I looked everywhere for you. For years. Everywhere. But you were smart. I never knew your real last name or where exactly you were from. Even with my money and connections, I couldn't find you. Even though my heart was heavy with the burden of my brothers' deaths demanding swift, sweet revenge, I could not fulfill the pledge I made to them."

His mood had made a sudden 180. His eyes were ablaze. Talking of his brothers focused him. His words spit forth with focus and anger.

"So eventually, I gave up my search. I decided to move forward, to not live in the past. You were a ghost. This was not an easy thing for me to do, Dan. But I did it, and I lived with it. Keeping it with me, yes, but buried deep."

He paused, mid thought, took a big breath in and sighed out, then looked me up and down. The anger that had filled his voice and eyes appeared to leave him.

"Life has been good to both of us, no?"

I finally found words. "I guess it has," I said softly and without emotion.

Where was he going with this? Had I lived in fear for no reason? Had he really come to terms with what happened and moved on, not caring about me or what had happened? Was his anger so easily satiated?

"But now, here we are. Doesn't this, this re-acquaintance demand that we re-examine the past and the future? You built your life off something that didn't belong to you. You took my money," he paused, looked around the store, lowered his voice and leaned in.

"You took my money." His voice was clear. Every word was like a bullet finding its mark. "And my product. You left me and my brothers for dead, took what was ours, and fled like a common thief. You must have known I was alive. You sold my drugs from my own house! My house!"

He yelled those last two words, which drew the attention of the dozen or so people in the bookstore. They looked up at us and then away. This was New York after all, and whatever was happening here was none of their business and not worth getting involved.

It came as a bit of a surprise that he knew I had sold his coke out of his house, and my expression must have betrayed my thoughts.

"Yes, I know," he nodded, smiling a pleased smile.

"I found that rat and made him talk. He told me all about the deal you gave him." Roberto took a deep breath and exhaled long and slow, while running a hand through his hair. He was working hard to stay calm. The anger was back. He was trying to control it. I was still unsure where this was all headed, only because we were in public and I knew that even though he wanted to strangle the life from me with his bare hands, he wouldn't do it here.

"It is true what I said, Dan. I did bury this and put it all behind me. I came to grips with what happened. The past was an empty, bad memory for me that I walled off in my mind and my heart. I no longer care to think about it, to go in that room inside my head. But today has changed that. Running into you—knowing that you are alive—the door to that room is again open. I cannot change that. I cannot change how I feel now."

If there had been copper wire running between the mere foot that separated us, it would have been alive with the tense electricity we both now felt.

"I want my money, Dan," he said as he stared at me, unblinking, his face empty of any emotion.

"With interest. Let's say, oh, ten million dollars. That's what I want from you, Dan Griffin from Pittsburgh. Ten million ought to do it."

The words carried a sarcastic, threatening tone.

"That's insane Roberto and you know it."

"Do I? Do I, Dan Griffin from Pittsburgh? Dan Griffin, husband to beautiful Diane, father to young, smart promising boys Chris and Dave? Do I think it's insane? Really?"

The emotion was back. Anger with a hint of hatred. And righteousness.

"Here's what I do know," Roberto continued, after eyeballing me for a few, short seconds. "You took my money and my cocaine. You left me and my brothers for dead. What you have now, all of what you have; your life, your wife, your family, whatever business you do or own, it is all because of me and what I allowed you to have that summer. And when it went bad, you didn't try to help me, save me. No, you left me for dead and took everything I had left as I lay there on that hotel floor."

He breathed in and out again. A giant, slow breath.

"Do you understand me? What I'm saying?"

He paused again, this time barely long enough to inhale. "You are what you are because of me. And that is worth something. I'm guessing it is worth a lot to you, Dan. I know it is worth a lot to me."

"I want ten million dollars," Roberto said again.

"That's crazy," was all I could mutter. My world was caving in.

"Oh, it is a lot of money, sure. But it buys you a lot. It buys you thirty years of living what has obviously been a very good life. It buys you all that—the past. But it also buys you the future. Because I promise you, Dan Griffin of Pittsburgh, if you do not pay me this money, this fee for allowing you to live this life, I will step on you like a bug."

"Fuck you."

Roberto laughed and threw his head back. "Fuck me? Really? You knew me well. You know what I'm capable of. You know how I live, what I do, how I repay debts and wrongs done to me. Do you think I have changed since you knew me? Do you think I am a reformed man, a law-abiding man? A calmer, gentler version of my former self? Is that what you really think?"

He ran a hand threw his hair and brought it down to his face, wiping away the wisp of sweat that had been building on his upper lip.

"You pay me $10 million dollars and we never see each other again. You can go back to being the ghost you were. Go back to your life and your family. Go back to what I'm sure is a beautiful home."

He paused again, lifted his right hand and pointed at me. "But you don't pay me? You don't pay me, and I come to Pittsburgh."

His extended finger was making his points in my chest now. He was tapping me in my chest as he spoke.

"I come to your home." Tap.

"I rape and kill your wife in front of you." Tap.

"Then I skin your boys alive. In front of you." His finger was stabbing me in the chest now.

"If you have pets, I do the same to them."

I grabbed his finger without breaking eye contact. He continued on just the same.

"Then I will cut you to pieces. And before you die, I will set your home on fire and leave you in it to roast."

Spit was flying out his mouth as he spoke while the volume of his voice steadily lowered. This was the old Roberto I knew and feared. The man who talked low but whose words were matched by unflinching violence.

"I will wipe you and everything about you clear from this world, Dan Griffin. It will be as if you had never existed. I will make sure that you truly are a ghost."

He broke free of my grip and took a deep breath in, exhaling as he looked around. His eyes eventually locked on mine and he smiled.

"Is that worth ten million dollars to you?"

Chapter 14

"Hey, there you are. Did you two have a nice talk and catch up a little?" Diane asked casually as I sat down next to her and the boys at our gate. She obviously hadn't been looking close enough to catch our body language.

Our flight was scheduled to leave in about forty-five minutes. I had been standing nearby at the adjacent gate for a few minutes after my confrontation with Roberto, watching my family go about their lives from a distance without the slightest clue of the danger they were in. The danger that I had put them in through the ignorant, unthinking actions of my youth. What had I thought would happen? Did I really believe I could avoid the past forever?

"Uh, yeah, we got caught up," was all I could muster.

"Wasn't that something running into Roberto?"

"Yeah, that was something, alright."

"What a blast from the past. Why haven't we ever talked about him?"

"I don't know," I lied.

"Well, I want to hear all about Roberto and what you two did down in Miami."

"OK."

I was staring off into the distance, not engaged with Diane in conversation, still numb and in shock from what I just experienced.

"Well?" Diane asked.

"Now?"

"Well, yeah, why not now?"

"I think I'm gonna grab a drink before we head home. I'll tell you all about it on the plane, OK?"

I turned and looked at Diane. She had a look on her face that appeared to say, *why is this such a big deal? Tell me now. Why do you need a drink?* Or maybe she just thought I was being odd, or just tired and out of it after the long transatlantic flight. Either way, she nodded and said, "OK. I'll grab a quickie with you," and took hold of my arm and lifted herself out of her seat.

"We'll be right back boys," she said over her shoulder as we walked off to a nearby airport bar. "We're just grabbing a quick drink. Our plane leaves soon, so you two stay put."

The boys nodded quietly, not looking up, absorbed in their video games and texting friends.

Once we were seated at the bar, I didn't waste any time. Before the bartender had finished introducing himself, I rattled off my order. "Grey Goose on the rocks with a couple olives, please." The drink was a clear, long established signal to Diane that I needed to catch a buzz in a hurry.

She glanced over, raised an eyebrow, and ordered a vodka tonic.

Turning to me, Diane asked, "So, this is just a wild ass

guess, but I'm going to go out on a limb and say you didn't like Roberto back in the day as much as he claims?"

I really wished that drink would hurry up and get here.

"Let's just say we left things on a bad note."

"That's it, a bad note? That's all I get?"

"No, that's not all you get. I'm going to tell you the entire story."

Where was that drink?

"There's an entire story? Oh boy!" she said with mock delight.

Diane was facing me and tapping her fingers in a fast tap, tap, tap staccato in frustration on the bar, waiting for what she assumed ought to be an easy answer. She may have been expecting something along the lines of competing for girlfriends or getting drunk and puking in someone's car. For the life of her, she had no clue how big a deal this was, how big a deal it was for me to finally come clean and how big a deal it would become for *us*.

I dreaded telling her, not for what I did, but for keeping what I did a secret from her all these years. We had shared everything. We had an open, honest, and wonderful relationship. I had made a conscious decision to hide not just what happened in Denver from her, but what I did for a living that summer and with whom I did it. I had hid Julie and my past from her. Afraid that telling her about my love for Julie and her death would tarnish or diminish our own love. I'd hidden my drug dealing from her, afraid of what it would say about my lack of moral fiber and character in my younger days, and whether or not that blind spot was still there. Ultimately, I'd never told her early on because I was ashamed, and because I was convinced she would leave me if she knew the truth about me.

I'd thought it through in my head hundreds, if not thousands of times since we first met. I'd *almost* told her dozens of times in the weeks leading up to me asking her to marry me, and dozens of times more before we were married. But the shame of my actions and fear of her reaction stopped me cold each and every time. Shame and fear—and the hope that I'd gotten away with not having to tell this tale led us here. And ultimately, I told myself that it was something that would never come up, so why dredge it up and create an issue where there was none?

Now, thirty years later—twenty since I met her—I was at a point at which I seldom thought about the past. I had come to believe I would never have to bring this up to anyone. I was being forced to come clean, and hope that Diane would understand the behavior from my youth that even I could still not wrap my head around—and hope she would forgive me for keeping these secrets from her and for lying to her.

If we were to be together forever, sharing everything, she deserved to know, even now when telling her meant I would be hurting her, and us. If she loved me like I believed, she would not pass judgment and leave. She would understand that I had made foolish decisions in my youth and that things had gotten terribly out of hand. I couldn't have been expected to make rational decisions after that bloodbath. And once those decisions were made, I had to live with them and build off them.

Mercifully, the drinks came. Diane looked at me expectedly and raised her glass, "Here's to whatever is coming." She said, now expressionless and evidently beginning to worry.

"Indeed," I said, as our glasses clinked.

After an awkward minute pause with the two of us just looking at each other, I began to speak.

"So, here's the deal Diane. I'm going to tell you something that I have been holding

back from you because I was afraid of what you might think of me as a human being. I did some bad things a long time ago. With, and for, Roberto. I was also afraid that telling you would bring a cloud of fear down upon you like the cloud that has been hovering around me for the past thirty years."

"Come on, quit yanking my chain," she said, smiling nervously. She took a sip of her drink, obviously hoping this was a big bullshit laden diversion to a much simpler story—or some sort of joke or put on.

"What I'm going to tell you is all true, Diane. I'm going to tell you everything and hope that you understand, not just the events, but my hiding these events from you all these years, even though I don't fully understand myself—and I pray that you still love me afterward."

"Shit," was all she could mutter quietly, taking another, longer pull on her drink. It seemed like she was beginning to believe this was no line, put on, or bullshit.

"Yeah, so here's the deal; Roberto was a big-time drug dealer in Miami. He ran cocaine. He may even be a bigger deal now than he was back then. I worked for him. I was what is called a mule. I moved large amounts of cocaine from Miami to Denver."

"Fuck."

"Yeah, and this is the short version."

"I'm going to need another drink."

"We'll both need another drink in a minute." I took another sip of the drink in front of me and continued my story. "I didn't do it alone. I had a partner. Her name was Julie. We were pretty young, like nineteen, but I loved her. We were kindred spirits in a crazy, fucked up high octane world of danger, drugs, and money."

"You were in love?" Her voice was quiet, but it didn't hide the shock and surprise she was feeling.

"Yeah."

"Double fuck," was all Diane could say. Her eyes were locked on mine now.

"Life was fun," I kept going. No sense stopping now.

"We were rolling in money and living the good life in Miami. We had it all under control, until we didn't. On a run to Denver, Roberto and his brothers made a move to take out the middle men—the guys, Jules and me…"

"Wait, Jules?"

"Yeah, that's what I called her."

"Jules, same name as your dog Jules?"

"Afraid so."

"Awesome."

There was an awkward pause, and then I just continued. "Roberto and his brothers made this move to take these guys out…"

"What do you mean, take them out?"

"Kill them. Roberto was—is—a very violent man."

"Did you kill someone Dan? Did you ever kill anyone?" She blurted the question out in a panicked voice, now suddenly aware of the gravity of what I was telling her.

"No. Never. I am telling you the complete truth. I've never killed anyone."

"But you were a drug mule for some crazy cocaine kingpin?"

"Yes."

She downed what was left of her drink in one gulp and made eyes with the bartender that a second drink was needed urgently.

"And you were in love with your drug mule partner, Julie… Jules?"

"Yes. Julie and I were in a hotel room with the middle men when Roberto and his brothers made their move. It was bad. Really bad. Everyone but us had guns. Everyone— EVERYONE was shot."

"You were shot?"

"Yes."

Diane was looking at me wide-eyed. Her jaw hung open in shock. No words, not even exclamations of "fuck!" were coming from her lips. This was not something that she ever expected to hear from me. Not ever. And I could tell from her face that she knew clear well that what I was telling her now was indeed what happened. The truth. The sad, gospel truth.

"That weird scar on your arm?"

"A bullet hole. When the smoke cleared, we were all laying on the floor. Julie was dead. It looked like everyone, everyone in that room but me, was dead. There was blood everywhere. Julie and I had been in some tough spots and we were prepared for dealing with bad situations, but this was beyond anything we ever saw coming."

I stopped to take a long pull from my drink. I put the glass down empty.

I waved at the bartender. "I'll take another, too."

We heard our flight called. They were beginning to board. The boys had stood up and were waving at us. I waved back and gave them the thumbs up, flashing a half-hearted smile to let them know we were on our way—even though we weren't.

"Julie was killed instantly. I'll never forget what she looked like lying there. And I'll never forget leaving her there."

"You left her?" Diane said the words in a loud whisper. Her tone somewhere between flat and incredulous.

"I had no choice. I left her. I left everyone. We were in a very public place and the police were coming. I was afraid. I didn't want to go to jail. They were dead, and I decided on the spot that I had a chance to escape. But if I wanted to get out alive and not face a life in prison, I had to act quickly. It was a bad scene, Diane. The worst. You can't imagine."

"No. I can't."

"Everything happened so quickly. It seemed like dozens of gunshots, all at point blank range. I was deaf from the noise alone. Smoke and blood filled the air. Bodies and blood were everywhere. I had been shot in the arm, but it wasn't life-threatening, so I bandaged it up quickly and got the hell out of there."

"You were shot." It was more of a statement than a question, as if somehow still not believing what I was saying.

"Yes. It wasn't that bad, all things considered."

"Jesus."

"There's one more thing I need to tell you now, so you see the whole picture. So you get why I never talked about Roberto and why I never wanted to see him again."

"Oh I get it, he's a drug dealer from your past…"

"It's more than just that, Diane."

"And he killed your girlfriend…"

"Listen to me. I'll tell you everything—whatever you want to know—when you're ready to hear it all, but right now, I need to tell you one more thing. One more very important thing, so you understand about Roberto."

"What?"

"After I bandaged myself up in that hotel room, while the alarms in that place were still ringing, and with all those bodies lying there on the floor all around me—bodies I assumed were all dead, including his—I packed up all the money and the cocaine from the deal that were there, and I took it. Sure, I had made a lot of money from Roberto that summer already, but that day, in that room, I took his money and his cocaine and left what I thought was his dead ass body behind."

"Only he's not dead," she half whispered the words as our flight was called a second time. The awful truth, the terrible, big picture of it all was now beginning to come into focus.

"No, he's not. I had figured that out pretty soon after the shootout. Which is why I high-tailed it back to Miami, got all my things in order, sold his coke, and got all my money together and blew town. I got the hell out of there as fast as I could and ran away. I ran away Diane. I hid out in the Adirondacks for two years, hoping my trail would go cold and Roberto would stop looking for me."

"And now he's found you."

"Yes."

"He's found us."

Diane's voice was dead flat now.

"Yes."

"He knows where we live."

There was no emotion in the words as she spoke them. They just sort of trailed off. The cold, awful realization of what I had just told her and what it meant had grown and blossomed in her mind like a mushroom cloud.

"He's going to come for us and kill us, isn't he?"

"Not if I can help it."

Chapter 15

The few people who knew the Villa brothers were travelling to Denver—and there weren't a lot of folks on that list—figured they were all dead once they heard the news about the shootout in the hotel there and its apparent tie to drugs. And they did what most people do when they hear news like that about people they know—they talked about it. By the time Roberto got back to Miami, a day and a half after the spectacular bloodbath in Colorado, pretty much everyone in his drug dealing, murderous circle knew about the shootout and presumed Roberto and his brothers were involved and dead.

Knowing how this crowd thought and acted, it really shouldn't have come as too much of a surprise to Roberto that when he walked through the front door of his house, his home was crowded with a dozen or so people from that circle. People who were partying and taking an inventory of the Villas' goods and dividing everything up amongst themselves.

Likewise, it shouldn't have come as too much of a surprise to anyone in the house at that moment—who shouldn't have been there—that if one of the Villa brothers came strolling through that front door alive, their reaction to them being there wouldn't be anything short of swift and murderous.

And so, another piece of the fabric of Roberto's myth was sewn that day. Bandaged, bloody and weary, he was nonetheless prepared when he came through that front door. After all, Roberto was hoping, more than expecting, that he would find Dan in his house, cutting his coke up or perhaps, miraculously, anxiously awaiting his arrival so he could give him back the money and coke he spirited away to protect it from being confiscated by the cops. One scenario was a pipe dream, the other, a fairy tale that only lived in his imagination. Roberto knew in his heart that Dan wasn't holding his goods until he could come back and collect them. He had stolen them in a panic and made a run for it, hoping to pad his bank account with Roberto's stolen money and drugs. On one level, Roberto understood the move completely. It was a smart play.

And while he didn't expect the throng of lowlifes and wannabes assembled like vultures in his living room when he walked through the front door, it was more than fair to say that their shock in seeing him alive was more than his in seeing them. It was also a possibility that they hadn't planned for.

He opened the front door, looked around at the scene before him, and without a word, pulled his brother's spare .44—which up until a couple of minutes ago, was tucked away in one of the Land Rovers—from his waistband and began firing canon shots into the crowd before they had a chance to react.

The first few shots sent people and blood everywhere. They moved like a flock of birds frightened by a loud noise, cramming together and moving in unison towards doors in a struggle to get out and survive. As if in a circus arcade, bodies went down like metal targets, one after the other. No one had time to reach for their guns and return fire. They were too busy scrambling to save their lives as thunder rang out and chunks of flesh flew through the air.

He stopped shooting and looked around. The house was quiet. Those who were able had escaped; diving out windows or doors—whichever was nearer. The less fortunate lay before him—six bodies spread in various contortions on the tile floor. Three were dead outright, sprawled about with big, gaping holes in their bodies. The other three were writhing, wiggling and moaning—shot, stunned and bleeding. He reloaded his gun as he walked slowly through the house looking for stragglers. Satisfied there was no one left, he tucked it back in his waistband and pulled out a smaller caliber Glock for the close in work. He sized up the survivors to see who might be able to talk—he wanted to take as much time with each to garner as much information as possible. The first man he approached was barely coherent and had little to say, so without so much as a word being spoken to him, Roberto put a single bullet in his heart and moved on.

Having seen how quickly he dispatched the first man, the second man he walked up to was much more talkative and had a very interesting tale to tell. It seems he purchased a large amount of cocaine yesterday afternoon inside this very house from a man whose description fit Dan's.

"Listen to me man," he pleaded. "I had no idea that coke was yours. There is no way, NO WAY I would ever have bought it if I had known that. No way!"

Sergio was in the early stages of begging for his life. Spit was flying from his lips as he spoke. His eyes were wide with fear.

"You have to believe me. Please."

He had a large hole in his left leg and was bleeding pretty badly. He'd taken off his belt and was starting to apply it like a tourniquet to help stem the flow but was having only marginal success. Roberto gave the belt a good tug, which brought out a loud scream.

"Of course. You would never do anything like that." Roberto said in a flat, unbelieving tone as he gave the belt another yank.

"I have seen you here before. What's your name?"

"Sergio," with a groan.

"Now listen to me Sergio," said Roberto, in a voice that was growing lower and quieter with each passing word.

"Listen carefully, because I need complete honesty from you. Honesty is good, do you understand?"

Sergio was sweating almost as much as he was bleeding.

"Yes."

"I need to know everything about your little transaction yesterday. You tell me the truth, tell me what I need to know and maybe you will get out of here alive."

"Yeah, yeah, sure." The words came out fast and panicky. Sergio looked over at the man Roberto had just shot dead and saw a chance to not be the next to be killed and grabbed it like a life jacket in an ocean of despair.

"So tell me, this man you bought the coke from here yesterday, was he anyone I know?"

"Yes, yes, the Anglo, the one with the pretty blonde girlfriend."

"Dan?"

"Yes, Dan."

"And the coke? Was there a lot?"

Sergio's trembling was more like a full body shake now. The combination of blood loss and heart-stopping fear almost too much to contain. He licked his lips, but no words came out.

"Was. There. A lot?" Roberto spoke the words slowly and loudly in a staccato rhythm, accentuating each word as he said it.

"Yes," Sergio shot back instantly. "Yes. It was a lot. Yes." Sergio said, nodding his head with each yes, now in total surrender.

"Pounds and pounds of it, Roberto. I paid him a hundred thousand for it all." His fear made him talk faster, like a record on a turntable that was slowly gaining speed.

"A hundred thousand?" Roberto asked in disbelief.

"Yes."

"That's a very good deal you got for yourself."

"Yes."

"Did you stop to wonder why he was giving you such a

good deal?" Roberto brought his voice back down to that oh so low and dangerous level as he spoke. Those who knew him well knew it was the slow burn of the fuse, the lull before the explosion.

He had started the interrogation standing and slowly had moved to a squatting position. Now, as he leaned in, his face was mere inches from Sergio's. Their eyes were locked. The only sound in the room besides the two men talking was Sergio's labored breathing.

"I did. I did. I asked him why he was giving me such a good deal and he said he had to get out of town fast. That I was paying him what he had paid for it and that he needed to get out of here fast and only wanted his money back on the deal."

Leaning in even further, in a voice barely above a whisper, Roberto asked "Did he say where he was going to in such a hurry?"

"No."

"Are you sure, Sergio? This is very important."

"I am sure Roberto."

With their faces mere inches apart, both men now spoke in near whispers.

"I am positive, because I asked him where he was going in such a hurry and he stopped and looked at me with a crazy look in his eye and asked me if I wanted this deal or not. He told me he could just as easily sell the coke to someone else and that what he was doing and where he was going didn't matter. That all that mattered was that the coke was for sale, and either I wanted it, or I didn't."

"And then what?

"I bought it. It was a steal."

Roberto pursed his lips and nodded his head understandingly.

"Yes it was. A steal."

He turned his attention to the third wounded man, who was sitting up, holding his bloody shoulder and watching the conversation with quiet, wide-eyed interest.

"What is your name?" Roberto asked him.

"Juan."

"That is a good name, Juan. I like it."

Roberto looked back at Sergio and then at Juan.

"Juan, you are a lucky man. I am going to let you live today. But only on one condition."

"Anything."

"You must leave here and tell everyone you know what you saw here today. Everyone but the police, of course."

His voice had begun to rise in volume as he spoke, from a whisper to thunder. It was only a matter of seconds until lightning struck.

"They must know that a man cannot steal from me, Roberto Villa," he said, his voice now booming and echoing off the walls.

"I understand."

"That I am a man to be feared. That if you steal from me, I will hunt you down and kill you." The statement was punctuated with a loud slap of his hand on the cold marble tile.

Sergio's body recoiled.

After a brief pause, Roberto raised his hand and pointed it him. He continued his rant, eyes now locked on Sergio's.

"That to cross me, even unintentionally, is to die for that sin."

Sergio's entire body now was trembling beyond control and he was mumbling something inaudible. Prayers probably. He knew what was coming. A barely intelligible murmur escaped his lips. He was begging for his life.

"Do. You. Understand?" The words, slow and loud, were as much a statement of what was to come as they were a question.

"Yes." Juan said, looking Roberto in the eyes and nodding his head.

Sergio's body was quaking. He was sobbing loudly and uncontrollably.

"Please Roberto, please, please forgive me." He sobbed.

"I did not know the coke was yours. I would never do anything to hurt you. I would never steal form you. Please don't kill me. Please." The words spit forth in full sobs.

"Shut up Sergio. Do you take me for a fool? You come to my house. MY HOUSE," he was screaming now.

"You come here and buy MY cocaine. My brothers died for that coke. Their blood is on your hands now."

"No…"

"YES. You stole that coke, Sergio. Stole it from me. From my family. In my own home."

He reached down and grabbed Sergio by the hair on the left side of his head, jerking his whole body. He held his head firmly and turned to Juan.

"Tell everyone this is what happens when you cross Roberto Villa."

He had quietly put down the Glock and pulled the .44 from his waistband while he talked. Held barely two inches from Sergio's head, the explosion was deafening. The flash of light, sound, and smoke so intense, it was as if it came from a battlefield. In an instant, Sergio's head was gone, with only a wisp of hair, scalp, and bone still held firmly in Roberto's hand. Sergio's body fell limply to the floor with a sickening thud.

"Leave," was all he said to Juan.

Chapter 16

Picking up the pieces of a drug empire once you're presumed dead and gone and out of the way, isn't an easy task. But it is much less difficult once word gets out that you're not dead, and that in fact, you're back in town and just happened to have gone on a homicidal rampage, blowing people to smithereens in your own home. Your competitors, enemies and even your friends tend to take notice of something like that, step back, and give you some room to move about back on to your old playing field.

So for the moment, Roberto had an open field, but he had no blockers, no team. Carlos and Juan were gone. And even though he was previously very clearly the brains and often the brawn of the operation, the Villa machine was just as reliant on the organizational and clean up abilities of his brothers.

Roberto ended up cleaning up his own mess that day in 1982—literally hosing down the inside of his house, wrapping the bodies in plastic and dragging them to a waiting Land Rover, and then hauling them down to one of his brothers' favorite dumping grounds in the Everglades.

Blood-splattered draperies and pieces of furniture were cut down, taken out, chopped up, and put in his outdoor fire pit and burned. The day long exercise reminded him of many of the valuable lessons that he had learned and applied to his drug business early on but had more recently been delegating. He would once again need to personally apply these moving forward. At least until he was fully operational.

Basic guidelines would suffice. For starters, don't be afraid to get your hands dirty. Or your house, or your car for that matter. Just be sure to clean it up really well.

Even if you ran the whole operation, you were never too far removed from a man with a machete or machine gun and you'd better know how to handle them when they came at you—and you better not be afraid of the clean-up. This wasn't accounting or retail, it was drug running. You surrounded yourself with unsavory characters who sometimes had to be dealt with in an even more unsavory manner. Dealing with it more than came with the turf —it often *was* the turf.

"If you haven't heard a man beg for his life within the past month, you're probably not being tough enough." He used to tell his brothers.

Roberto built his empire back, deal by deal, piece by piece, month by month. With his brothers gone, he was responsible for making sure his entire operation worked smoothly. From purchasing to distribution, from money laundering to settling turf battles and everything in between—it was all up to him. And while he had never been hesitant to apply violence to his competitors, and anyone who owed him money—he found himself solely in charge of everything, and there was nothing he was unwilling to handle as he re-built. From pulling the trigger, to putting the shovel in the ground, to disposing of anything or anyone in order to regain and retain his business's standing and success moving forward.

Likewise, while he had gotten used to operating the machinery from the top and setting up the deals that brought in the Villa cocaine and distributed it; the bookkeeping, banking and laundering had typically been done by his brothers. After Denver, he was forced to handle all of those tasks that had previously fallen to Juan and Carlos. Eventually, he came to rely on no doubt less trustworthy lieutenants to care for some of those day to day operations that he didn't have the time or interest in, but that was just one of the new rules of engagement he had to get used to. The unwavering level of trust he had in matters he wasn't personally involved in was gone. Trust had to be earned and would never truly be given completely to a lieutenant who wasn't related by blood.

Holding what was left of Sergio's head in his hands that day in his living room, Roberto had another stark realization. That while he had no doubt that he was up to the challenge of what lay ahead, and that success would again be his and his drug empire would reign supreme over South Florida; happiness would elude him until the wisp of hair, scalp and bone held in his hand belonged to Dan.

Revenge was both a physical and a mental need. It burned inside him. As the days turned to weeks and the weeks to months after the Denver dust up, the need to find and kill Dan grew more intense, if less reasonable. It began as a goal, then became a need and slowly evolved to an obsession. He paid dozens of people to find scraps of information about Dan, but no one was lucky or good enough to draw him nearer to his mark, and no lead was strong enough to develop a direct link to where Dan had fled or vanished. Roberto personally combed through the hotel pad Dan and Julie called home that summer in hopes of finding anything that could point him to where Dan might have retreated. But there were no clues to their past there, no tells on where they came from, where "home" was or where Dan might flee, now that his world here had crashed and burned.

Dan had once said something about a grandmother in Upstate New York—a small town near Syracuse—but in the pre-Google era, without knowing the exact town or Dan's last name, the squad of killers he sent there had no real chance and turned up nothing.

All Roberto's informants were sadly coming up empty. They found nothing in Miami either—Dan had been careful not to ever disclose personal information nor to leave scraps of it around for anyone to remember. The one and only person who could have delivered the kind of information that Roberto would have used to trace Dan—his banker—had decided life in South Florida was too fraught with peril for his liking and had left in a hurry for parts unknown by the time Roberto's henchmen came knocking. He left no forwarding address.

All these dead-end leads were a source of huge frustration and aggravation for Roberto because while his number one immediate goal was to piece his business and his life back together, his number two goal was to find Dan and make him pay for the situation he now found himself in—starting over, alone, with his brothers dead.

Because even though it was his own greed that hatched the plan to travel to Denver to ace out the yuppie middle men in his operation there and take over the entire drug trade, and it was his own trigger finger that sparked the gunfight that left his brothers dead, Roberto still blamed Dan for being the hiccup in that plan that caused it to fail. He had convinced himself that if Dan were not there—had not been in that hotel room, his plan would have succeeded, and he would now be entrenched in Denver and his brothers would be alive and helping expand his empire there and points further west. He was sure it was Dan who had turned on him and tipped the yuppies that danger was literally at their door, eliminating the element of surprise. Dan may have just as well pulled the trigger himself and killed his brothers.

And most importantly, it was Dan who had not cared enough to confirm he and his brothers were dead or alive. It was Dan who methodically stole his cocaine and his money. It was Dan who stepped over all their bodies to beat a hasty getaway.

If he had simply taken a cowardly retreat and left the drugs and money, Roberto would have let it be. It would have been explained away as the mindless, panicked actions of a man in shock. He could understand that. And he would now have his coke and his money.

Instead, Dan stood there amidst the death and destruction and calculated a cold, selfish, greedy, disloyal action plan that stripped him of his property and left him for dead. When he turned that around in his head, over and over, Roberto went to a very dark place.

Of course, if he had thought through the reasons for his anger with a cool head and honest viewpoint, he would have thrown himself into a fit of depression and melancholy with the realization that it was his own greed, stupidity, and brash actions that filled the hotel room air with hot lead and cold blood. That it was he and he alone who was responsible for the deaths of his brothers, the Colorado yuppies and Julie. His strategy hatched the plan and the plan set actions in motion. His plan, as if it were his own finger on a trigger—once pulled, spewed death. An honest, thoughtful inventory of his emotions and actions would have left him in a place he was probably incapable of surviving, a place where he shouldered the blame for the carnage and the deaths, a place where he was to blame and not Dan. So instead he shifted that blame and placed himself in the role of the vengeance-seeking brother who would never stop until Dan was found and dealt with appropriately.

In the weeks immediately after the shooting, Roberto withdrew into his house, becoming a virtual recluse. No one came by to check on him—no one in their right mind would dare to after what he'd done upon his return from Denver. Alone with his thoughts, his fears, and his dreams, the days turned to weeks and the weeks to months. He slowly began to come to terms with his predicament and forge a plan to move forward. By late in the second month, he had begun to come out of the house and walk the neighborhood and the beach. He began eating and drinking in the local restaurants, coffee houses, and bars. At first, he stayed to himself, but eventually he began meeting with people, finding acquaintances, and forging renewed and new relationships with people with shared interests.

Roberto the recluse had determined life was worth living. That it was better lived socially with others and that it was best lived at the top of the food chain, with his desires and bank account full. It was time to rebuild his life and his organization. Time was something not to be squandered or misspent. That lesson had been taught to him with unflinching violent pragmatism and he understood that whether he wanted to or not, that it was time to move on. What was, was. What is, is. And what will be has not yet been determined. That was something he *did* control.

He began taking meetings with some of the other young Cuban Americans who had grown up around him, who were several years younger than he was and who looked up to him as a Miami legend and hero of sorts in their community. They'd seen him as one of their own, and as someone who had managed to pull himself up to the top of the heap using nothing but his own guile, smarts, and brawn.

From the ones he deemed to be the most loyal, smart, and driven, he handpicked a cadre of dedicated criminals and forged new partnerships. These men swore their allegiance and loyalty to him. It wasn't family, but it was the next best thing and absent his brothers, it would have to do. These people felt a communal tie—working with him was like growing up to work with one of their childhood heroes—it made them proud, even if what they did was against the law. While his informants combed the state for clues that might someday help him find Dan, his lieutenants worked to strengthen his Colombia to Miami network, build a new bridge to Denver and to construct a local network there. He still believed there was a lot of money in those mountains and he planned on getting his share.

Bringing his Columbia to Miami trade back up to speed was no problem. His Columbian partners really never knew that he was out of the picture and once word got out about the bloody welcoming home party he threw for himself, they were even more impressed with him than they had been and began to consider him a blood brother of sorts. Any would be competitors in South Florida simply stepped aside or moved to another territory rather than to compete with Roberto head on.

Taking over the Colorado yuppie trade, as it turned out, was also easier than he first imagined it would be while dreaming and strategizing about it during all those lonely, hermit-like days licking his wounds in his house. The Denver bloodbath managed to eliminate the only real, substantial cocaine network in the state. Three months after the Denver shoot out, Roberto took a handful of his new lieutenants on a field trip there to ascertain whether getting a foothold in the booming yuppie coke market was still feasible and discovered to his surprise, the market was wide open and waiting for him. He had taken out the only local large-scale coke dealers anyone there knew of. There were no roadblocks to him building a new network from scratch.

He stayed nearly two weeks in Colorado, spending time in Denver, Telluride, Breckenridge and Aspen—all places where wealth and excess leisure time equaled a desire and demand for what he sold. He and his team searched out street dealers and moneyed yuppies in highbrow bars, restaurants, clubs and gyms, and eventually found enough people with enough interest and money to make a new Colorado enterprise a viable endeavor. He decided to leave two of his new Florida associates in Aspen to set up shop and solidify connections. The others would fly back with him and help build a new mule system similar to what he had developed with Dan and Julie to ferry his product and cash back and forth. Only unlike the old system, he would control both ends of the pipeline this time. There would be no middle man. No gun-toting Colorado yuppies. The excess profit he had dreamed of earning by selling his coke for street retail instead of middle man wholesale would make him millions instead of hundreds of thousands each month.

It didn't take long to come together. Six months after the shootout, the entire operation was up and running and churning mounds of cash. Six months after that, Roberto branched out to Los Angeles, building a similar distribution system there, and within two years he was the single largest and most profitable cocaine dealer on the continent. His network was extensive and well-managed. He had reached out, nurtured and established an equally envious network of banks and bankers to handle the millions in cash he spun each month and had used those connections and that cash to purchase dozens of restaurants, car washes and coffee houses to launder his money. He even bought poor Chris Harris's construction company.

Roberto's enterprise was big and successful. Costs were high, but profit margins were ten times the most successful legitimate business operating anywhere. The L.A. "office" alone, in its heyday, with its high-end, needy Hollywood clientele, spun nearly ten million in profit a month. If he were a mainstream, legal businessman and the Harvard Business School had done a review of his strategy, systems and execution; he would have been deemed a genius, and he would have been a Fortune and Rolling Stone cover boy to boot.

As with any other business, he contracted in slow times and expanded in the good—as business and political winds necessitated. Unlike other businesses, he invested a fair amount of his resources in staying out of jail and eliminating unwanted competitors with ruthless focus and violence. He developed and maintained a vast network of police and judges who were also on the payroll and helped smooth out or eliminate hazards and threats.

Some of the lieutenants he brought on after the death of his brothers were killed in skirmishes, others received a death sentence from Roberto for crimes against him and his code. But the majority of the two dozen men he recruited and trained early on, had stayed on to become wealthy and remained loyal and with him decades later—eventually becoming his new family and support system. And as the years wore on, Roberto's empire continued to succeed on a level and scale that most people couldn't comprehend. He stayed clear of the battles and violence associated with trading heroin, crack, meth and other drugs and remained focused on maintaining his grip as the biggest supplier of cocaine. Roberto was proof there was genius in knowing your strengths and staying true to your mission and brand.

Often, supply and demand forced him to make changes in product, quantity and price, but the cocaine business was resilient and always seemed to be booming and flush with cash. His network stretched from coast to coast. This new "family" headed up his efforts in Denver, L.A., New York, and Toronto. Miami was the hub and central office for the operation and it continued to be from there that Roberto managed the overall conglomerate.

For all the little things that Roberto did right to make his operation run smooth, the true secret ingredient to his longevity and success was his understanding that he needn't be too greedy. The Everglades, slopes of the Rockies and the Hudson River were filled with the bodies of upstarts and competitors who weren't able to follow that simple tenet.

At some point over the years, he had the realization that the wealth he had acquired—that anyone doing what he did for as long as he did—was so immense that he truly had no way to spend it all over the course of an extravagant lifetime. And that realization freed him to think and act more clearly—which ironically, brought in even more wealth by clearing the way for continually expanding not just the reach and resources of his illegal network, but by also expanding the pace of his purchase of and investment in many legitimate businesses as well.

He had all the cars, homes, toys, and beautiful women he could ever want. Even so, he flew First Class, rather than purchase and operate his own personal jet—which he could easily afford. That would only draw attention and likely, scrutiny from federal agencies he'd rather stay clear from.

So it was that thirty years after the Denver shoot out, he found himself walking through that terminal at JFK, thinking about grabbing a coffee at Starbucks and killing time while waiting for a flight back home to Miami that he spotted a man that looked strikingly similar to how he imagined Dan would look if he were alive today.

It was a game he often played with himself. Scanning crowds of people in far flung places, imagining the face and body shape of men and comparing them in his mind's eye to how he remembered Dan and how he presumed he might look today. There was hardly ever a man who needed a second, serious glance. But today's scan produced a man with such remarkable similarities that Roberto had stopped dead in his tracks and found himself staring at him in a near trance.

"Motherfucker," he mumbled to himself as he watched the man's movements. He was about the right age, and his body shape and size was exactly as he remembered Dan— plus about ten pounds. He watched the man talk to a woman who was a ringer for how he imagined Julie would look after all these years. The man's wife, from the look of how they talked and acted. And there were two teenage boys. He did the quick math in his head, adding the years and slowly nodding to no one but himself.

"Why the fuck not?" he asked himself, as he decided to make a closer observation. He sauntered up and by the man and managed to casually cross his path twice, coming within feet one time and nearly bumping in to him on his second pass.

Roberto's mind raced back and forth between the past and the present as he tried to paint two pictures of Dan and morph them together. His face grew flush, sweat beaded up on his upper lip and his heart began to race. It *was* him.

"You fucker!" He whispered aloud. "After all these years, I found you. You're mine."

He'd spent at least a quarter of a million dollars on paid informants, tips, and private detectives with nothing to show for it over the years. Nothing. He'd been forced to give up on the hope of ever finding Dan alive. While deep down he remained quietly obsessed with him, he'd finally come to grips with the stark realization that the man was a ghost he would never find. He'd kept the frustration buried deep until today, when by sheer, happy coincidence, he found himself virtually face to face with that ghost—in the flesh—shopping in a bookstore at the airport.

He'd traveled the world over. From the outside looking in, he had everything a man could ever want. But inside, he was incomplete. There was emptiness, a longing, a need that was unfulfilled—a painful longing that all that wealth and the passage of time could not dull.

And that need—in his very core—was to find, torture, and kill Dan. And here that man was, thirty years in the waiting, standing before him casually looking at books and magazines in an airport terminal. He was nearly speechless. Nearly.

After a moment's long pause, standing still and silent while his mind raced one last time to completely confirm and then grapple with the truth in front of him, he moved.

Walking up behind the man he was now convinced was Dan, he leaned in close enough so that his lips were mere inches from the back of the man's head and whispered in his ear.

"What chew doing, mang?"

Chapter 17

I used to love sitting on my back deck looking out at the world north of Pittsburgh. It was calm, peaceful, and serene. With my big, beautiful house behind me and the rolling hills stretched out before me, the rich landscape gave me a feeling of warmth, community and security no matter the season. This was my happy, comfortable and secure world, and there was nothing here that was beyond my understanding and control. But that was no longer the case.

As I sat here today and looked out, I felt trapped, as if in a prison of my own creation. This world of mine had been built upon the ashes of a false dream—born from sullied money, obtained illegally, controlled not by me, but rather by a vengeful ghost from my past who had suddenly burst into my dream world and demanded to take all that was mine. He demanded my attention, my fear, and my money.

My money or my life, and the lives of my family, to be exact.

If only it were that simple.

I actually could come up with the cash. I had started with a big chunk after all, saved, invested smartly and saved some more. I had the ten million—and more. Coming up with the ransom in exchange for the lives of me, my wife and children, wasn't unreasonable—and I was prepared to do it quickly. Sure, it was a shitload of money, but it was money well spent if it got the job done.

But that was a BIG if.

Instead of thinking, *Holy shit, how am I going to come up with that impossibly large chunk of cash*, I was thinking, *What happens after I do?*

Roberto had clearly carried the weight of his vengeance across time and I imagined nothing short of him exacting it fully would likely soothe the pain in his dark soul. The money was just icing on the cake. A little something extra to make the wait worth the effort. The cash was the gift. I was the prize.

Knowing how Roberto thought and acted thirty years ago was a window into how his mind likely worked today, and that knowledge quickly convinced me that no amount of money would save my life. He had wanted me dead then, he wanted me dead today, and he would want me dead tomorrow.

Maybe he would spare my wife and sons if I gave him the ten million, but there were no guarantees with Roberto on things of this sort.

Oh sure, he would gladly take my money. His made-up ransom sum would go a long way toward covering the initial sum worth of what I had taken from him, plus the compounding interest over thirty years. But it wasn't as if he needed the money. He looked like he was still successful, rich and powerful, and if he'd continually grown his business over the decades, ten million was an insignificant sum to him.

Roberto had likely plucked the number from the sky as we spoke. He hadn't been carrying it around with him all these years, hadn't been working rolling averages daily. He merely made it up on the spot because it sounded big enough to about cover what a man might deem worth waiting thirty years for. It sounded large enough to be worth the lives of me, my wife, and my children. It sounded large enough for me to have taken the bait. And I had—hook, line and sinker. But what choice did I have really?

The sliding glass door opened, and Diane walked out with a portable phone in her hand. Trembling and pale, she handed it to me. Her voice, barely audible, confirmed the call I'd suspected would be coming, had arrived.

"It's him."

I ran my hand down her arm gently, lovingly, while maintaining eye contact as I took the phone from her, mouthing the words "It's OK."

She stood there, frozen in place by fear.

"Yes?" I spoke clearly and unemotionally.

"What chew doing, mang?" Roberto asked jovially in his best fake Cuban gangster voice.

Despite decades to prepare, I wasn't ready for this. Maybe I never would be. But I had no choice but to confront it head on. Our lives were on the line. I took a deep breath in and exhaled slowly, calming myself as best I could, and put up a brave front.

"What's the deal with that fake, bullshit accent Roberto? Does it scare people or impress them?"

"Ha, ha, ha, Dan. Yes…" Roberto said drolly, in long, accented syllables. "It does both. You don't like?"

"It doesn't do either to me, Roberto. I know you."

"Then you know what I am capable of," he stated flatly, changing his tone instantly from friendly to threatening.

"Don't you, Dan Griffin?"

He was using my previously unknown last name as a spear to poke me with. To show me, with just one word, that I was no longer safe.

"You know this part, this banter, is just for show. Just to make what must be done fun," he paused.

"For me, not you," he added, laughing to himself. It was the laugh of a man who knew the extent of his power and his reach and took enjoyment from instilling fear and hopelessness in his prey before bringing the hammer down. I said nothing while he performed.

"There is no bullshit, no fake anything in what I have said to you and what I expect from you, Dan."

He paused again for effect.

"I have been quite clear in what I expect from you. I expect you to pay me ten million dollars in exchange for your life and the lives of your beautiful wife and children."

He paused much longer this time. Perhaps five seconds. I was doing all I could to maintain my calm, not reacting— or overreacting. Taking deep breaths, I listened intently, while staring expressionless out into the hills. Diane's hand had been resting gently on my shoulder but was beginning to clench and grab hold.

"Are you still there Dan? Are we clear?"

"Yes Roberto, we're clear."

"Ah, good, I could tell from our brief meeting in the airport that you have grown to become a man of reason. That comes with age, no? And with experience and success. You've had all three, Dan, haven't you?"

Where was he going with this psycho-babble? The price had been set. I was going to pay it. Let's just get on with it.

"I have gained all three also, along with much wealth and power," he added, not waiting for a response.

"That gives a man like me much ability in this world of ours."

"I'm happy for you, really I am," I said sarcastically.

"So, know this also Dan," he continued, clearly no longer acknowledging my snide comments. He had something he wanted me to hear.

"This is no time for you to be a smart ass. No time for you to overthink your options and try to deceive me in some childish way. This is not a time for you to act dramatically without much forethought as you did that day in Denver. This is no time for rash actions or decisions, Dan. No time for foolish bullshit."

"Great, thanks for the advice, Roberto."

"No problem. You see, I have done some research on you since the day we met in the airport, Dan. Some checking up. You might go so far as to say I know pretty much everything there is to know about you—except where the fuck you went when you left Miami and dropped off the face of the earth with my money and cocaine."

I exhaled long and deep. This was angry Roberto. If we had been face-to-face, I would be seconds from a mortal blow, a gunshot to the gut or having a garrote slipped around my neck from a soft-shoed associate sneaking up on me from behind.

"I know you have done well for yourself, Dan. That the ten million dollars is something you can get your hands on in short order. So, I want the money delivered, via bank check—in person—this Thursday at a place of your choosing in Pittsburgh."

"Thursday?"

"Yes, Thursday. Let's be honest Dan, you could have it today if you needed to. I need to delay it a few days though so that I can arrange my own travel plans and schedule. I'll be accepting your money in person."

Good grief.

"There's no need for you to bother yourself, Roberto. I can wire the money to the bank of your choosing. We never have to see each other again." Roberto was an animal. I could only hope my fear wasn't palpable. Like a lion in the wild, he would sense it and pounce, setting his jaws upon my jugular.

"Oh, but we do. There is much to catch up on."

"No, Roberto," my voice rising slightly, Diane could hear both ends of the conversation from her close perch and began to tremble more and stepped back from me.

"There is nothing for us to catch up on."

"That's where you're wrong. I want to hear all about your

life—the ups, the downs, the loves—how you escaped from that hotel room. Was it difficult washing Julie's blood from your hands, Dan? Do you dream of it still? Do you still dream of Julie?"

"Just take the money…"

"I am a curious man, Dan Griffin. I want to hear it from you, in your own words. Maybe over a cup of espresso, like the old days!"

Roberto chuckled to himself again.

"I want to hear about your pretty wife and handsome sons, too. Are they there with you now, standing by your side?"

"Let's not do this."

"Or do they not even know the truth yet, Dan?" Roberto's voice was upbeat and playful, but the words were meant as weapons.

"Please…"

"Oh, so that's it. The boys know nothing at all, and let me guess, Diane found out after we chatted in the airport. Is that what that serious discussion was over drinks before you caught your flight home to Pittsburgh?"

He'd been watching me for a reaction and saw it for himself.

"You're a bastard, Roberto."

"Yes, there is no doubt of that Dan. And there is no shock value in that to anyone who knows me either. But this new revelation you laid on your loving wife—talk about shock and awe."

"We're done here."

"Does Diane know how closely she resembles Julie? How you loved that woman? How you led her to her death and how you held her lifeless body in your arms and sobbed? It ruined you, Dan."

His psychological barbs found their mark. He was peeling back scabs I had forgotten about.

"You had to disappear from the world—not just from me—you had to disappear from everyone and everything to get away from your grief and despair, didn't you? To wash the blood away. To wash the memory away. You needed to vanish from everyone and everything to cope. To survive. That's no secret, that's obvious. You weren't just running from me, Dan Griffin. You were running away from the world."

My jaw hung open. My throat was dry. His attack was vicious, unrelenting, and uncannily spot on.

"But now I'm back, Dan-O, back in your life." I could hear what sounded like a snap of the fingers or his hand slapping a chair or table.

"I'm back in your life, and the memories of those good old days with me are flooding back, aren't they?"

"I'll make the arrangements, Roberto. You'll get your money."

He kept on his attack, not responding to me.

"And your boys, so handsome, so young and full of life. Do they know that the blood of others is on your hands? That you dealt drugs, and stole my money and drugs when you were but a few years older than they are now? What kind of role model are you?"

"We're done here."

"Are we?"

"Yes, we are."

I gathered myself as best I could. Trying to sound like his words held no power over me. When I finally spoke, I spoke as firmly as possible.

"Thursday afternoon. 3 p.m. There's a coffee house called the Bee Hive on East Carson Street on the city's Southside. It's busy, public, and cops love the place."

My heart was racing. I expected Roberto to say no, or to yell, or laugh—anything. But he was silent.

Finally, he said, "Thursday. The Bee Hive. It will be splendid seeing you again. Goodbye." And with that, Roberto hung up.

I set the phone down on the side table and looked up at Diane. She had stood by my side for the entire phone call— close enough to hear Roberto's voice booming through the earpiece of the phone. She walked slowly over to the deck's rail. Leaning on her elbows, her face slowly melting into her hands, she looked sad and desperate. Who could blame her? I stood and walked over, putting my arms around her to show my love and appreciation for her being here for me. Her body went rigid.

"We're going to get through this," I said in as calming and reassuring a tone as I could muster, even though I couldn't fully believe it myself.

Her head slowly swung side to side, as if she were about to say "no."

Instead, "Fuck you, Dan," came out in a near mumble,

as if she'd been thinking it and hadn't fully intended for it to be mouthed out loud, her head facing the woods. It caught me by surprise, but not nearly as much as what came next.

She spun around on her heels quickly and unexpectedly and slapped me hard across my face. It was the first time in twenty years of marriage and courtship that either one of us had laid a hand on the other in anger.

"Fuck you," she said again. There was no mumble this time. The words were more of a roar. She followed the insult up with another swing, hauling off with a right-handed slap. I caught this one in mid-air.

"What the fuck is that for?" I asked in disbelief and shock.

"Really, you don't know?" The words shot out. Her face was red with anger. Her eyes were glistening and filling with tears.

"Well, no, not exactly," I stammered.

Sure I knew I was responsible for the jam we were in, and I knew Diane was seriously upset over it all, but we hadn't really had a heart-to-heart since our airport sit down. I had assumed—apparently incorrectly—that she was somehow coming to terms with this whole crazy situation and trusted me to figure out a way to handle it and make everything OK.

"This whole mess is your doing."

"Yes, I know," I said, nodding.

"What kind of person were you, Dan? What kind of person are you?"

The words cut into me. My stomach clenched as if I was

in the throes of food poisoning. Twenty years of love up for grabs because of a lie—or rather—a truth I'd never come clean on. I needed to plead my case.

"You know me, Diane. I am not some other, evil person. I'm the guy you know, the man you love, the father of our children, a good father and husband who always has and always will take care of you and the boys."

"But that isn't adding up, Dan. I heard the whole conversation you just had with that madman. You were a drug dealer. You hung around drug dealers and murderers. And you were in love with another woman. A woman who was also a drug dealer and who apparently looked just like me and who was murdered because of your mistakes."

"That's not exactly true."

"Which part isn't true?" She was trembling again, the anger and hurt bubbling up in tears and running down her cheeks as she spoke.

"You weren't a drug dealer? You weren't in love with another woman—a woman I wonder now—that you were trying to replace in your heart, with me?"

"No, Diane, nothing could be further from the truth…"

"No? You got her killed, Dan. You."

"No."

"It sure sounds like you did. Then you mourned her. I get that. But then you replace her with me?"

"No, no, no…"

"And now this crazy, fucked up past of yours comes crashing into our lives and you're going to get me killed, too! Did you ever love either one of us? What about the boys?

Will you get them killed, too?"

The words stung worse than anything Roberto was spouting on the phone. I stepped back away from her and looked her in the eyes.

"That's not what's going on here, Diane. That's not who I am." I spoke the words firmly and calmly.

"But that's who you were. You were that person. Even if you tell yourself something else now to make you feel better inside, you were a drug dealer. You did bad things. You were a bad man."

She stopped talking and didn't say anything to me for a full minute. We stood there just two feet apart, but it might just as well have been a great canyon separating us. Tears were still rolling down her cheeks. My guts ached.

After a couple of minutes, I stepped in slowly and put my arms around her tightly. She struggled against me, fighting back at first, pushing back, not wanting to connect physically, but I pinned her arms to her sides as she squirmed, wiggled, and groaned.

"Stop. Stop it. Stop it." I said quietly and lovingly, over and over.

"Shhh."

Her protests started loudly but slowly quieted down. Eventually, she took a deep breath, buried her face in my shoulder and after a minute, started crying softly. Slowly, the crying turned to a sob. Big, body-wrenching sobs sent her chest heaving up and down. It went on like that for a couple of minutes. I gently ran my fingers through her hair and eventually, as she calmed, I began to talk gently and tenderly.

"I was a kid. I was nineteen and looking for adventure. I wasn't a drug dealer. It was the adventure, the adrenaline, not the drugs that drove me."

She let me hold her, and we both needed that. I needed to talk to her and explain myself to her, and what I believed I needed to do now to save us all. She needed to hear my words and be reassured these years weren't all a lie, and that I had a plan that could help us out of this terrible bind we were in. I needed her to be on board and work with me, be part of my team.

"Look, I told you what happened thirty years ago," I began.

"You were a drug dealer," she said, not letting me finish my sentence. Her eyes and words cold, her face expressionless. The crying had stopped, but Diane was far from understanding how I kept this secret from her all these years.

"A drug mule to be exact."

"I was young, restless, and too smart for my own good. I took some time off from college, found my way to Florida, and hooked up with a girl in Miami I really liked. We were having a good time and started hanging out with a crowd of serious partiers."

She was listening finally.

"Roberto was in that crowd. He had a magnetic personality—lots of charm, money, cocaine and pot. It was a fun, easy crowd to hang out with. I was a partier back then. Julie was too."

"Julie. The girl who looks just like me," she said flatly.

I kept going, ignoring what could be something that

would drag this conversation in a useless direction. I had to get this all out—fill in all the important blank spots I had left out when we talked in the airport. We needed closure on the past, so we could deal with the present.

"We were inseparable. We were young, had time on our hands and liked to live on the edge. We ended up spending a lot of time around Roberto and his friends. There was always a party going on and it was fun—it didn't seem dangerous—not at first anyway."

"Do I want to hear this?"

"You need to hear this," I said in a calm, serious, deliberate tone.

I paused for a brief moment, and then continued.

"Roberto had always told Julie and me that we were a cute couple. After a few weeks, he pulled us aside and told us that we were naturals—and that that sort of thing—that sort of real deal was an important ingredient in what made his business succeed. There was nothing fake about who we were when we were together. That's when he gave us the pitch about his business and about moving drugs back and forth between Miami and Denver. He told us that our naturalness around each other would be part of a perfect, easy disguise and that that was worth a lot to him. If we joined him, we would have more money than we ever imagined."

I finally had Diane's full attention. I took a deep breath and kept going.

"Jules and I knew Roberto and his pals were always rolling in cocaine, but I guess we never took the time to think it through, that people with that much money and drugs were probably not just buying it for themselves but were dealing it."

"Jules? How comfy."

"We WERE comfy, Diane." I said it forcefully, but not with meanness. I had to make her understand that we were tight back then, that we were in love and that what happened tore me apart, but that I wasn't carrying a torch for Julie now and that I didn't marry her in some misplaced emotional screw-up.

"It was thirty years ago, Diane. Ten years before I met you. What went on then wasn't about you. And you are not about that. I'm telling you all this, so you understand what I did and who I was—and hopefully, that you'll understand that who I am today is not that same person I was then."

"OK," she said quietly, nodding as she walked over to a chair and sat down. I had her full attention. It wasn't a nod of approval or even understanding—but rather—one of acceptance.

"He wanted us to join his team. He'd shown us exactly what needed to be done—and explained that it was a job that only a couple like us could pull off—oh, and he emphasized again that he'd pay us handsomely to do it. We were his connection—his mules—who took his product, that's what he called it, product, from Miami to Denver, where we traded it for cash."

"How much?"

"Kilos each time. Over ten pounds."

"Jesus," she said under her breath.

"We'd tape it to my body and fly commercial airlines, acting as a couple. Then we'd meet his buyers at hotels around Denver and trade the coke for cash, ship the cash back on an overnight delivery, fly back to Miami, pick up the cash, and bring it to Roberto."

"How much money?"

"Hundreds of thousands each time. Usually six to seven hundred thousand dollars."

"Jesus Christ."

"Yeah, it was a lot of money."

"How much of that would he give you?"

"Twenty-five thousand dollars apiece, every time we took the trip."

"Holy shit. How many times did you do it, take those trips?

"Over fifty."

"Fifty!"

"Yeah, fifty trips. Twenty-five grand each time, apiece. So now maybe you can understand, at least a little, how a 19-year-old kid might get caught up in thinking that was a pretty cool, easy lifestyle."

"That is a shitload of money," Diane said shaking her head, almost understandingly.

"Yeah, it was. Still is. But we were pretty smart about how we dealt with it all. We spent enough to live well, but saved almost all of it, really. We knew we had a good thing going—even if it was crazy dangerous—and that it wasn't going to last forever. After a couple of months, we knew the lifestyle wasn't for us. Roberto's crew ran fast and hard. We figured we would work through the summer months and then get out and be set for life."

"Why did he need you—why did he need anyone? Couldn't he just have his own planes and people go back and forth with the drugs and money?"

"He didn't want planes and all that infrastructure. He wanted people—people he could control and trust."

"What was he like back then, Roberto?"

"Most of the time he was very likeable, and he was like a brother to us. He was smart, funny, educated. He treated us like family. We hung at his house a lot but made sure we kept our own space too. Because as nice as he was to us, we'd seen him be brutal with others, so we knew what he was capable of. He was a ruthless businessman. We saw a lot of bad shit happen to people. If you crossed him, he and his brothers would fuck you up."

"What were his brothers like?"

"Roberto was clearly the boss, the older brother that they looked up to, followed and adored. They could be killers but that is not what defined them. They'd come from nothing in Cuba and were humble. They were cool, I liked them. They weren't as colorful as Roberto, not by a longshot. They were quieter, more laid back. They handled the money, the books and some of the connections. And they cleaned up after him when he went off on people. Roberto really couldn't have operated as big an operation if they hadn't been there, I guess he's figured out how to do that now without them."

I hadn't thought of that before. The brothers really had

been the backbone of the operation when Julie and I were involved. Roberto's operation now appeared to be bigger and even more sophisticated than the one he ran when we were in it. He'd evolved. Interesting.

"Were they violent too?"

"Oh yeah. Maybe not as boisterous or braggadocios as Roberto, but they were just as dangerous with a pair of pliers, a knife or gun, and wouldn't hesitate to hurt or kill you if it served their interests."

"Oh my god. Did you see any of that, were you involved in any of that?"

Diane was now engrossed in what I was telling her, and I think, wanting to believe that I was not the ruthless, heartless thug she feared I might have been earlier.

"We didn't see it directly because we avoided it. But we saw plenty of people pushed around and moved into a private room or the garage, from which we'd never see them again. The Villa brothers killed with impunity. Dozens of people. They'd bury the bodies and evidence in the Everglades."

"Oh my god."

"Yeah, we'd seen enough of that to know that getting out would be tough—getting out alive, anyway—so that at some point, we knew we would have to disappear, just vanish from that place in order to survive it."

"Is that what you did? Is that why you did what you did? Take the money and the drugs?"

"Yes, and no. I hadn't planned on doing it then and there, but I felt like I had no choice because of what happened."

"What did happen, Dan?"

I took a deep breath and let out a long soft sigh.

"The Villa brothers—who hardly ever left their safe confines in South Florida—appeared unexpectedly at our hotel in Denver. They strolled right up to us while we were taking our contacts to the meeting in our room. I never really knew why they were there, but I assumed they wanted to run the entire operation and were there to take out their Colorado partners. Take them out and move in."

"Take them out?"

"Kill them."

"What? Why? Why would they do that?"

"Greed. Instead of selling wholesale to them, they would torture them, learn about their business and supply chain, kill them, move in and take it all over—and then sell retail to the masses. They were there to literally take out the middle man. Roberto had likely run the numbers. They'd make millions more on each shipment. Millions."

"Wow. So what happened?"

I'd certainly thought about what happened a lot. Run it through my mind thousands of times. But I'd never really been forced to talk about it out loud—the shootout, Julie's head exploding all over me, being shot. I'd spent years in the mountains—originally hiding not just from Roberto but from the reality of what happened, and eventually I'd come to some sort of uneasy terms with it all. But I never had to say it out loud to another person. Never had to voice it. To explain it so tactically. I became unexpectedly emotional.

"This isn't easy to talk about, Diane. Not this part. It was and is the most awful thing that has ever happened to me."

"I think I understand, Dan. But I still need to hear it, I'm sorry."

I took a long, deep breath and let it go. I talked for thirty minutes straight. I described the shootout, Julie's dead body, how I patched myself up and got out of there. I told Diane all of it, including my escape from Florida and how I set the money accounts up. I explained the truth behind what she and my sons called my little "cabin in the woods" and about my remorse for what happened; for my naïve, youthful, unrealistic belief that what I was doing was just some sort of "playtime" that I would walk away from, unharmed and unscathed.

I talked about my impressions of Roberto the man— then and now—and what I thought was the emotion, frustration, and anger that he took with him over these decades and what I thought he wanted today.

When it was over, Diane stood up and walked over to me, taking my head in her hands.

"I am sorry for all the pain you went through. You were just a little boy, really, caught up in a man's world. You're so very lucky to have gotten out alive and to not be emotionally scarred."

"You don't think I'm scarred from it all?"

"You were, but you somehow managed to accept what happened and bury it. It never got tangled up with who we are or who our family is."

It was her time to talk now.

"Ultimately, what we have is awesome. We're going to

have to get through this and maybe afterward, talk about all this more so I can fully feel comfortable with you again. But I'm even more amazed than ever that we somehow found each other all those years ago and have managed to carve out this great life together."

It was my turn to be speechless.

"This is fucked up, Dan. Really fucked up."

"Yes. Yes, it is."

"But I still love you."

I stood up and hugged her hard, like I haven't in years. We stood there on the back deck like that for a long time, my head buried in her shoulder, smelling her hair and her scent and loving her more than ever.

"So, what are we going to do about Roberto? He won't be happy with just the money, even though it's such a large amount. He won't be happy until you're dead—maybe, until we're all dead."

She'd heard me, believed me and now fully understood the mess we were in and what we were up against.

"I know," I said after a long pause and another deep breath.

"I know. But I've got a plan."

Chapter 18

Roberto was as happy as a schoolboy packing for a long-anticipated summer beach vacation at the end of the school year, as he laid out his clothes and gear for the trip to Pittsburgh. Khakis? Check. Rain jacket for the always present threat of Pittsburgh rain? Check. Comfortable shoes, credit cards, and spending cash? Check. Handguns, shotguns, automatic machine guns, knives, ropes, duct tape, and plastic ties and body bags for torture and murder? Check, check, check, and check. And he made sure they were also bringing his favorite new toy—a sleek, small drone equipped with a GoPro camera for surveillance. Nothing said "surprise attack" like aerial reconnaissance.

The sun was streaming in through the long, bullet-proof windows on the second floor of his mansion as he finished packing. He was listening to rhythmic Buena Vista Social Club songs on his iPhone, which connected via Bluetooth to his in-house surround sound system. His hips were swaying, and his feet were tapping as he went about his business. He was in an upbeat, happy go lucky mood, and why not? His thirty-year blood quest was about to conclude with his quarry caught and killed. He'd spent years thinking about what he would do to Dan once he found him, and now that that day was finally here, he was gladly ready for the inevitable torture, murder, and dismemberment and burial. What self-respecting drug lord wouldn't be in a great mood?

There was a knock at the door to his bedroom suite. It was Victor, his most trusted lieutenant.

"Roberto, we are packed and ready," he said respectfully.

"The plane is standing by, fueled and prepped. We wait for your word to move."

Victor was the most focused, most clever and most deadly of all his aides. He would accompany Roberto in Pittsburgh, along with two other exceptional members of his inner circle, Domingo, and Fortunato. All three were Cuban-born American citizens, and like most of Roberto's trusted associates, had a four-year degree from the University of Miami thanks to his benevolence. UM was a school rich in Cuban tradition and he was happy and proud to pay tuition for dozens of young sons and daughters of Little Havana each year with no expectation other than the guarantee of his city's quiet support of his unlawful enterprise. A side benefit was that the brightest students would graduate and pour their talents back into his adopted neighborhood and day by day, go on and make it a more prosperous place in which to live. Even drug dealers had a soft spot in their hearts.

Of course, some of those students would also come home from college to find gainful employment with him. Victor,

Domingo, and Fortunato—like so many other poor, young Cubans growing up in Little Havana—had idolized Roberto as a hero. They saw someone who had come to America, carved out a life with a successful, dominant business, who readily and regularly paid it forward to his Cuban community. To graduate college and go to work for him was a respected, feared, and honored profession in their community, and all three were fiercely loyal and proud to be a part of his organization. Roberto had built a new family support system to take the place of his dead brothers.

"I'm almost ready. Load the car, I'll bring my bag down in a minute."

He liked to run through the list of necessities he was bringing on a road trip one last time before departing. There was nothing worse than having to shop for toothpaste, deodorant, or a decent razor while traveling. What was the use of all those tens of millions in the bank if he had to use a plastic, throwaway toothbrush?

Roberto had gathered his troops and laid out his plan immediately after hanging up with Dan. He would fly to Pittsburgh as soon as possible, scout out Dan's movements and actions and get the lay of the land of the terrain there. Especially the areas around Dan's home and the Bee Hive. He'd dealt with many an adversary who thought they'd gain the upper hand by drawing him into their lair and springing a surprise on him. The surefire way to defeat such a person was to surprise him with an unexpected, intimate knowledge of their own back yard and have a little surprise of your own up your sleeve.

There would be no commercial airlines used on this trip. His travels needed to be secretive; his movements invisible. Renting a private jet from a trusted business associate would allow him to pack all the firepower he needed without worrying about pesky airport TSA personnel, or having to purchase guns and ammo from unknown local thugs in Pittsburgh.

Pleased with his pack job and his plan, he walked downstairs, set the alarms, and closed the big front door behind him. Victor was at the wheel of one of his Land Rovers. Domingo and Fortunato road in back. Before he jumped in the front passenger seat, he gazed around at his beautiful home and out over Atlantic Avenue and the Ocean beyond one last time.

He'd made a good life here. He had more wealth and material goods than any man could dream of, he'd traveled the world several times over and had surrounded himself with beautiful, desirous young women. He'd provided for his people and community. This was a home he built and loved. Perhaps when this business with Dan was finally behind him it would be time to find a woman who was his equal and to marry and have children of his own. Family was the only missing piece to his legacy.

He'd think it through when he returned.

He'd never been to Pittsburgh before, but it was as rainy and dreary as he had feared it would be. Google had told him the region was near the top of the list of the most overcast and rainy cities in the nation, a far cry from the sunny Florida weather he'd known most his life. He zipped up his rain jacket and put his brand-new Pirates cap on his head to shield himself from the drizzly raindrops as he stepped off the plane. He was pleased with his choice of clothes and shoes. He'd be comfortable here, and as small and seemingly inconsequential a thing as that was, it would enable him to keep his mind clear of petty nuisances and free for the more important strategizing and busy work that lay ahead, as well as any unforeseen surprises that might conspire to overtake him.

Google had also given him several historic, swanky hotels from which to choose from. He'd picked the Renaissance, a landmark building on the Allegheny River sitting on the edge of the city's theatre district. It was across from Heinz Field—home of the Steelers, and PNC Park—where the Pirates played and where he planned to take the boys to a baseball game and unwind a little while there. It was good for the spirit to mix a little pleasure in with business. It also didn't hurt that the hotel was just ten minutes away from the Bee Hive coffee house where he'd meet Dan later in the week. This town was dank and dreary, but it appeared to have a lot going for it despite the downbeat weather and seemed vibrant, nonetheless.

Once checked in, he treated Victor, Domingo, and Fortunato to an afternoon pick-me-up, coffee at the Bee Hive. The joint was crowded with twenty somethings, college students, hipsters and business types looking for free Wi-Fi. Creaky, old wooden floors, a hodgepodge of furniture from the 60's and 70's and eclectic, electric paintings and drawings that hung from the walls added color and atmosphere to the place. The espresso was good and the brownies delicious. What wasn't so good was the location. Dan had smartly picked a place that was popular and busy, and on a crowded, two-lane inner-city street that was packed with people, cars, and bikes. There'd be no public execution here—at least not one in which he and the boys would easily escape from. Taking Dan hostage here would also present major obstacles. They ordered coffees to go and spent the next several hours walking the streets surrounding the coffee house, hotel, and stadiums, casing the entire area for "what if" scenarios.

The next morning, they got up early, packed the drone in their rental car and drove fifteen minutes north of the city to the suburbs. Victor was again at the wheel as they drove slowly through the neighborhoods around Dan's home with Roberto by his side, taking in every house, tree, streetlight, and yard with keen interest.

Pittsburgh is one of those areas that is so nearly universally hilly, every home is on some sort of slope where the backyard either slopes up and away or down and away. Dan's house was a bit of an oddity, sitting on a mostly level piece of land. The front faced neighbors across the street, and behind those houses was a hillside—on top of which, perhaps a half mile away from Dan's house, sat another cluster of homes perched up high and looking down on Dan's street and home. His backyard looked down a long, wooded hillside and onto another neighborhood, also perhaps a half mile away. There were a lot of homes and neighbors, but there was also enough wooded open space and cover that Roberto felt that this was a far better hunting ground than the downtown coffee house area.

He'd call an audible and force the confrontation here, at Dan's. He'd take him buy total surprise.

"Victor, circle back around to that community down below. Boys, we'll drop you off down there."

Domingo and Fortunato nodded silently from the back seat.

"Snoop around. Walk the neighborhood and poke around the houses that back up to the woods behind Dan's. Look for dogs, fences, and any obstacles that could get in our way in the dark. And try to find some natural trails that lead up that hillside to his street and better yet, to his backyard. Walk it all. Get a feel for the terrain without raising suspicion."

"Sure," replied Domingo. "What are you thinking?"

"I'm thinking…" he paused as he gathered his thoughts. "That the coffee house presents too many unknowns and dangers to us. That this area represents a much better confrontation zone for us."

They all nodded quietly, in unison.

"I'm thinking those woods could be a good place to launch our surprise. Someplace we can quietly set up, gear up under the cover of night and slide up the hillside, then break into their house and take them all before they know what hit them."

"That sounds strong," said Domingo, everyone else nodding again in agreement.

"We're going to go up there," he said, pointing to the top of the other hill and the neighborhood sitting atop it.

"Victor and I will look around up there for advantages and obstacles. I'll put the drone up while we're up there too and get some aerial surveillance of the whole area."

Everyone nodded, liking what they heard. Roberto was a big believer in planning his work and working his plan.

"We'll get pictures and video of his house, the neighbors, backyards, fences—everything we can in this whole area— and based on what that all shows us, we'll map out our best approach accordingly."

"Sweet," said a smiling, normally quiet Fortunato.

"When you're walking around, don't just think about how we get in. Worry about getting out, too. And if you see something that might give us a better option than what I've mentioned, tell me."

Domingo and Fortunato nodded in unison, happy with being given such a prestigious task and to be a part of Roberto's attack team. It was an honor to be trusted with this, and they took it to heart.

"The drone will give us a wide, bird's eye view," he continued.

"Smart planning is a necessity, but technology can be a distinct advantage." He was always looking for an opportunity to reach and teach his lieutenants, to mentor them.

Within ninety minutes, Roberto had seen all he needed to see to feel confident he would finally get what he'd spent thirty years hoping for—sweet revenge.

Everything was beginning to fall into place. The terrain was mapped out and he believed the area would give him easy access to his prey. The aerial view from the drone revealed fences, culverts, dogs, and a score of other potential pitfalls and land mines, but it also showed several trails and yards that should give them the sort of quiet, hard to notice access they would need in a surprise attack.

His plan was coming together in his head. He was comfortable with it, his surroundings, and his team. He'd handpicked these lieutenants from among all the loyalists who worked for him and swore they would die—and kill—for him. These men were trained and experienced in these sorts of surprise raids and he had confidence they would succeed here. Unless Dan had an invisible electric fence, night vision cameras, and armed security guards, he would die in his own home.

A second, backup scenario was also crystalizing in his head. Life had taught him that possibilities and eventualities never materialized just as you imagined they would and that you needed to have contingencies ready when you were in the battle field. Being able to improvise was often the difference between succeeding and failing, living and dying.

By the time he and Victor drove down to the lower neighborhood to pick up Domingo and Fortunato, he was pleased he'd taken every possibility into account, and had a plan for each.

They had worked hard.

"Let's take in the Pirates game tonight boys. Some ballpark food, cold beers, and baseball under the lights—it's just what we need to get in the right frame of mind."

They had earned a break. The days ahead would be busy ones.

Chapter 19

If I could just stay alive until Friday—I kept telling myself—I will have likely survived whatever apocalypse Roberto had planned for me. And by doing so, I would also keep Diane, Chris, and Dave out of harm's way too.

If I could make the exchange and not be taken hostage, or tortured, if I could make the money exchange and negotiate my free release, if I could get my family away from here and to some safe place, where Roberto couldn't get to them—then maybe I could walk away with enough to provide for my family and have a safe, secure future.

Those were some big ifs. I'd need smarts, planning, and a shitload of luck to make it to the weekend alive.

And staying alive was of course, priority one, but not at the expense of everyone I loved. The more I thought it through, one fear that materialized as one of my greatest, was that Roberto's twisted, sick thinking might hatch a plan that actually intended to keep me alive but murder my family. Stripping me not of just the ten million in "ransom" he wanted, but of everything that I held dear. And as for the money, truth be told, I had socked away nearly twice as

167

much as he wanted. But it wasn't the personal wealth I feared losing the most, it was my family.

What better way to impress upon me the gravity of the loss he felt thirty years ago than to take my family from me? To make me feel his own loss, understand it and then leave me to live with my own loss forever, just as I had left him. I had to take precautions to ensure that would not happen.

I cleared my schedule at work for the week and blamed the surprise staycation on the need to stay close to home, while Diane made a quick trip to her parents to nurse a sick mother.

Assuming Roberto might come to town a day or two prior to our meeting to surprise me, I convinced Diane to pull the boys out of school and take them away someplace that even I was unaware of—so that if I was to be tortured, I couldn't give their location away and have my final, dying thoughts be about how I had signed their own death warrants. Diane would take them someplace far enough away and not near family or friends, where she could keep the boys occupied without raising alarm bells. If I were killed while they were gone, she knew how to access funds. She'd have to learn how to manage on the run.

"This is bullshit, Dan." Diane hadn't liked my plan when I first laid it out to her and had let me know how she felt in no uncertain terms.

"Bullshit. Do you understand? This is bullshit. We should be doing this together. I can help you. You shouldn't be doing this alone."

"Look, it's not like I'm thinking, 'Hey, I got myself into

this mess and I'm going to get myself out of it,' OK?"

"Then what is it?"

"I just don't want you or the boys anywhere near when this goes down."

"I understand not having the boys around Dan. I'm not an idiot. I'm your wife, not some socialite diva who doesn't know what it's like to get her hands dirty. I can handle myself and help you if things get rough."

She'd grown up with brothers, took karate as a teen, and knew her away around guns.

"I know you can, and I really appreciate that that's how you feel." Her face was flushed with anger. She looked beautiful standing there in our kitchen arguing with me.

"But you have to trust me on this."

I walked to her, stepped in close and took her hands in mine as I lowered my voice to a near whisper.

"Roberto is a murderous, conniving, vengeful bastard. If he gets us all together…"

"He won't, Dan, we're not idiots!" Her voice rising in anger.

"And neither is he." My voice rose up to match hers. I was growing frustrated and angry. I laid it out for her as plainly as I could.

"Listen to me. Roberto and his team—there will be a team—will come in armed to the teeth and will be unafraid to use any weapon at their disposal. They are trained, experienced killers, do you understand? Killers."

"Yes, but…"

I didn't let her finish.

"He will rape and torture you, and if he finds the boys, he'll torture and kill them. He'll have already tortured me to within an inch of my life and he'll have me tied up and force me to watch what he does to you all. He won't stop because of anything you, the boys, or I say or do. He'll only stop when he's tired, or bored. And then he'll kill you all— probably slitting your throats or clubbing you to death with a hammer. In front of me. Then he'll decide that's the worse fate for me—to let me live with those images in my head for the rest of my life."

Diane had stopped arguing with me—stopped talking. Letting go of my hands and taking a step backwards in a recoil as I spoke, she'd suddenly grown sullen and quiet as I described in vivid detail what I knew Roberto was both capable of and likely planning. She was visualizing what I had said. After a moment, she looked me in the eye.

"How do you know that's what he'll do? How do you know exactly how it will go down?"

I rubbed my face slowly with my hands. I hadn't really wanted to get into this sort of thing with her. Knowledge was power after all, and this revelation had the power to change how she thought about me forever.

"Because," I paused, exhaling, looking her directly in the eye. "I've seen him do it to others."

We stared at each other, just standing there in the quiet kitchen for a few minutes. I knew what horrible thoughts she was imagining, but I couldn't bring myself to say anything more. Sure, I could have gone into more detail, but knowing the specifics of that sort of gruesome violence was something I hoped she didn't need to hear. She only needed to know that I believed Roberto was capable of it still after all these years, and that we needed to steel ourselves against the possibility of that happening to us. With it all out on the table, there was really no reason for us not to do exactly as I said, and we both knew it.

After a few more minutes, Diane walked over, poured a glass of water from the tap, and sat down at the counter. She didn't need or want to know any more specifics.

"So then, what DO we do exactly?"

I laid out my plan in detail. I needed her to take the boys and leave the following day, Tuesday, and not come back until sometime next week. But looking online at their flight options, she realized the earliest she could get organized and book flights to wherever she would take the boys, was Wednesday morning. That still gave me a day and a half to retrace my steps and be sure I'd prepared for every eventuality. That would have to do.

We decided to split up some of the chores and get to work immediately. Diane started to pack for herself and the boys, with an eye toward being away about a week. I left to run errands and pick up some much-needed essentials.

I started with my bankers, with whom I'd managed millions and bankrolled dozens of projects over the years. When I called and told them I had a new project, they set aside what they were doing and jumped right in. I'd decided the bank check was a ridiculous idea and that the only way to safely deliver Roberto his ten million dollars was to set up his own offshore account. My bankers had set one up for me a few years back while I was designing a condo project on Saint Kitts Island in the Caribbean. It was a relatively easy process—I lied about the reasons I needed it—but it guaranteed Roberto would get all his money without any taxes or questions. It was more than a show of good faith— and I was counting on that to keep him happy and I hoped, give him at least one good reason not to kill me—after all, I was actually giving him his money, guaranteed, with no strings. Unless he pulled some shit on me first—and then I could keep the money—all my money, away from him.

With the paperwork done and the electronic transfer complete, I drove from the bank to a well-respected local gun store, where after careful discussion with the owner, decided on my weapon of choice—the Stoeger Double Defense Shotgun— a double barrel, single trigger, lightweight home defense deterrent.

I tried it out in the back room firing range, blasting away at cardboard human cutouts. It was light, easy to use and load, and even a novice like me should be able to hit my target consistently, as long as it wasn't too far away.

"Not bad huh? That'll stop a burglar or bad guy in his tracks," the owner said with a proud smile after I'd blown a hole in the middle of a cutout.

"Yeah, I should think it would."

"So, should I box one up for you?"

"Yes."

Rather than buy five "hunting rifles" from the same store and raise concerns and questions, I spent the next couple of hours driving to four different gun and outdoors stores and bought four more of the Stoegers along with boxes of shells.

The shotguns were lightweight, short-barrel, double-barreled and clearly packed a killer kick. Purchasing five of them would ensure that one was always within arm's reach, and that I would be able to instantly defend myself in case one of Roberto's thugs came blasting through a door or window. My intent was to have a few surprises of my own ready when Roberto or one of his gang came a knocking.

I also purchased a SafeGuard bullet and stab resistant vest I planned on wearing under my shirt to my meeting with Roberto. Even though I had picked a very public, high traffic place to make our transaction, I didn't put it past him to shoot me or have someone else shoot—whether we were in public or not. As long as they didn't put one in my head, I should be able to survive.

Tuesday began as a quiet, unexciting day. The sun came up peacefully this last day before my wife and boys left me for parts unknown to the outside world. Chris and Dave went off to school with their standard noisy, hurried departure. Chris mumbled something about an after-school meeting. Dave, the typical high school senior, had no such plans but wouldn't be home until supper regardless, choosing to hang with friends and girls rather than with the two of us. Diane and I were left lingering over coffee in the sunlit kitchen. If the specter of death wasn't hanging over us, it would have been a pretty nice start to the day.

I came up behind her as she was rinsing out her coffee

mug. I started nuzzling her neck gently while lightly running my fingertips across her shoulders, down her arms, onto her hips and down the outside of her legs. Her body was warm, smooth, and sensual. Her pleasant scent both calming and stimulating. This crisis had blocked out a lot of normal emotions and thoughts, so it was good to feel a stir in my pants as my heart began to pick up its pace.

"Anything special planned for the day?" I asked, with a smile.

She turned slowly on her toes, her body facing mine. She raised her arms up and rested them on my shoulders. As she lovingly ran her fingers through the hair on the back of my head, I felt goose bumps rise on my arms.

"Not until a few seconds ago," she said with a mischievous grin.

It was good to see we were both in sync.

We kissed gently, pulled back, looked deep into each other's eyes and kissed again, this time deeper and longer. We both felt a sexual stir. We added some gentle groping to the kissing and after a few minutes, managed to stumble, still entwined, into the living room, where we landed on the couch.

From meandering to urgent in a matter of minutes, we peeled each other's clothes off as if our lives depended on it. After twenty years of marriage and with a body still firm, supple, and youthful, Diane was as desirous as the day we first kissed.

Our lovemaking was fast, loud, and urgent. The exact opposite of our normal, nearly always planned bedtime trysts. It was exactly what we both needed to feel fully alive in the face of death.

We laid there for a few minutes afterward, panting.

"You're heavy," she said with a laugh, and with a quick turn of her body, a raised knee and a push, I was unceremoniously rolled off of her and the couch and onto the floor.

"Hey!"

I feigned disbelief. I wasn't the least bit mad, but instead was thrilled that we were able to pull back the near constant veil of dread and darkness we'd been living behind since our airport run-in with Roberto. The spontaneous fun was a delightful respite from the awful reality that I had been planning and preparing for.

"So, like I was asking before you ravished me, anything special planned for today, my love?"

She giggled a girlish laugh and threw her head back, then turned and looked at me with a semi-serious face. It was the sort of playfulness couples seem to have more of early in their relationships than after decades together, yet here it was. It was also exactly the kind of smart-ass comment Julie would have said at a time like that.

It surprised me that that thought would have popped into my head, ever, let alone then. Shocked me. Until recently, I'd buried all memories of Julie deep down in my brain for so long, I was amazed at the unprompted ease with which they popped to the surface. Sure, I'd been forced to think and talk about her in recent days thanks to Roberto, but I hadn't given her any deep thinking. Now, as I lay here doing just that only moments after I made love to my wife, the woman I'd been accused of marrying because of her resemblance to Julie, sent my mind racing.

I felt a sudden pang of guilt—both for even thinking of her at a time like this and for what had happened all those years ago. I'd spent years coming to terms with what happened in that hotel room. If I still couldn't convince Diane or Roberto that Julie's blood wasn't on my hands, how was I ever going to convince myself?

I pushed the thoughts out of my head.

"I'll help you finish packing for the boys, and then maybe we can grab some lunch."

"Really?" Diane asked with pleasant surprise. "I thought you had big plans today?"

"I just need to make sure my head is in a good place. That I am clear and focused on being in the moment, so when the time comes to meet and hopefully, talk and negotiate, I find a way to make this all work to our advantage. And if Roberto has other plans, that I am ready for that too."

"And how are you going to do all that?"

"I have some stuff to do around the house and then I'm planning on chilling out with you most of the day, getting a good night's rest, and being at the top of my game starting tomorrow."

"I hope it's as easy as that."

I doubted it would be, but I had to have a plan.

"It should be," I lied.

But after I'd loaded and concealed four of the shotguns around the house and one in my car, there wasn't much to do to get ready.

"Let's finish getting the boys packed and then let's go grab some lunch."

"Deal."

Chapter 20

Roberto and Domingo sat up straight in the front of their rental car. Both men brought small binoculars to their faces. There was movement far down the hillside on the neighboring street. A garage door was going up and a late model black Honda Accord slowly backed out into a driveway. The driver's side window slid down, revealing Dan behind the wheel with his wife Diane sitting in the passenger's seat. They were smiling and talking and appeared to be having a nice time as they drove away.

Roberto reached for his phone and called Victor.

"Get ready, they're leaving the house together."

"What kind of car?" Asked Victor, as he started the engine on the rental car—the team's second—which Roberto had impulsively decided to get just yesterday as he made last minute adjustments to their plan.

"Black Honda Accord."

"Not much of a ride for a big shot millionaire."

Roberto had thought virtually the same, as he and Domingo sat high on the hill overlooking Dan's house. They'd been there since sunrise, watching for movement, waiting for an opening. Victor and Fortunato sat just up from the neighborhood's only entrance, now with their car's engine idling.

"Follow them and let me know where they're headed and how far away it is," Roberto instructed.

"Gotcha." And with that, both men hung up.

Roberto was a fan of surprise attacks. A big fan. He was betting that Dan hadn't forgotten that about him—and considering what he'd lived through in Denver, why would he? So he anticipated that Dan was going to be prepared in any way he thought he needed to be—to do anything he needed to do—probably at least a day before their scheduled meeting. He knew Dan would attempt to be prepared and guarded against any unsuspected shenanigans. That's why Roberto decided to make his surprise move here, out of the blue, before their scheduled meet-up at the Bee Hive.

Dan and Diane drove past the dark colored rental without a second thought and pulled out onto the busy two-lane road that crisscrossed the neighborhoods. Less than five minutes later, they were seated for lunch at the local Eat'n Park.

Victor called Roberto from the parking lot.

"They're at a local restaurant. Looks like they're grabbing lunch."

"Tell me where?" asked Roberto.

Within minutes, both cars were side by side in the Eat'n Park parking lot. Roberto watched the couple through the window from his safe perch in the car. Sun streamed in through the windows, spilling onto them and making them seem bright, warm, and happy. Dan and Diane looked so calm, so natural. Not a thing out of place in their lives. Just a typical married couple out for a bite to eat.

Roberto signaled to Victor and Fortunato.

"Leave the car here. Grab your gear and come with us."

The Eat'n Park was right off I-79. No one would think twice about a car left parked here for hours, even for the better part of a day. Dozens of commuters did it daily.

All four of them drove together to Dan's house and pulled into the driveway. Roberto's instructions for Victor were simple and direct. "Walk around back and get in through the rear deck or basement, then come up and open the garage door. Don't trip any alarms."

The neighborhood appeared quiet, no one was moving about except for them. Victor got out and casually walked around the back of the house like he owned it.

Roberto trusted this lieutenant like no other. If there was a delicate situation that needed to be dealt with, a partner to be persuaded, a throat to be slit—or as it so happened, a home to be broken into—this was the man he relied on to get the job done quickly, quietly, and cleanly. There was nothing he couldn't or wouldn't do.

In less than two minutes, the garage door began sliding up on its track. Victor stood inside near the door to what looked like a kitchen hallway. When he made eye contact with Roberto, he smirked.

"Domingo, come with me; Fortunato, drive back to the restaurant. They should still be there. Call me to let me know they are and then stay and have a cup of coffee. When they leave, call me, and then start walking here. We'll leave one of the back doors unlocked for you. Leave the car in the lot with the other. We'll ambush them here and afterward, use their Honda to double back for our cars. We can't chance anything being out of place here. If they are already gone when you get there, let me know immediately and I'll give you other directions. Do you understand?"

"Yes," was the only word needed and spoken.

Roberto and Domingo got out and walked into the garage. The door went down as Fortunato pulled out of the driveway.

"I already called the school and told them Chris and Dave would be out the rest of the week on college visits."

"And?" I asked absent-mindedly.

"And nothing," Diane said, pushing the lone remaining piece of lettuce around on the plate in front of her as she spoke. "They said to enjoy it and wished us all the best of luck."

"Luck?"

"Yeah, it's the kind of thing they like to see high school kids take days off for."

"Oh yeah."

My head was elsewhere. I was trying to enjoy the day with Diane, but my brain had slipped back into self-preservation mode. Luck was something *I* was going to desperately need.

I paid the check and we got up and left, deciding to go

home and finish the packing for her and the boys before finishing last minute errands and purchases for the trip.

As we walked to the car, I noticed a young Hispanic-looking man behind the wheel of a car parked almost next to ours, eyeballing us from behind dark sunglasses, talking to someone on his cell phone.

"He looks suspiciously unsuspicious," I thought to myself.

"What? Who?" Diane asked. Apparently, I'd not only thought it, but said it out loud.

"Oh, no one," I replied, not wanting to alarm her unnecessarily.

I didn't like looking at everyone as a threat, but such was life until the real threat to us was past. I dismissed my initial concerns about this man, thinking I was over-reacting because he was Hispanic.

Still, I watched in my rearview mirror with a wary eye as we pulled out and headed home. He didn't follow us, and I put him out of my head.

The remainder of the short ride home was quiet. By the time we pulled in to the driveway, my mind was elsewhere—thinking about my upcoming face-to-face with Roberto and wondering how it was going to go down. Neither of us spoke, both lost in our own worlds of worry.

Part 3

Chapter 21

The garage door went down silently behind us as we stepped into the kitchen. I threw the car keys on the counter and walked through to the family room, stopping to look out the full-length windows and out across the valley that stretched away down the hillside behind our house.

"The sun may just stay out," I shouted out to Diane, who had walked past me and was heading up the stairs.

"That's nice. Maybe we'll have a good travel day tomorrow," she replied back over her shoulder.

"Hey, do me a favor," she continued.

"What's that?"

"Go downstairs and see if the boys have their nice, black and gold Steelers hoodies laying around down there and bring them up if you find them."

I chuckled to myself. Steelers hoodies would be referred to as "nice" or acceptable attire only in Pittsburgh, where following the team was more religion than sports fandom.

"Sure," I said as I began to turn around and head for the basement stairs.

"And shut that music off down there. One of them must

have forgotten to turn it off this morning before they left for school."

"Sure," I said on auto pilot, as I opened the downstairs door. I took one step down and froze in place.

The music was on.

For the life of me, I didn't remember it being on when we left the house. Why was it on now? The boys hadn't left the music on this morning. They never did. They hardly ever had time to come down to the nice, finished basement in the morning before school to play video games or listen to music. And when they did, it was the TV they left on, not their music. They'd always unplug their iPods and take them with them.

I took a step back up the stairs and retreated into the family room, opened the cupboard beneath the bar, and took one of the Stoegers out from its hiding place. I cocked it open to make sure both barrels were loaded and closed it, making a comforting click as I did. It is a stiff gun, and it made more noise than I wished it had while opening and closing it.

"Honey?" I yelled upstairs, holding my breath, hoping and waiting for an answer.

"Yeah?"

"Nothing." I exhaled. She seemed safe up there, away from this uncertainty. That was good. There was nothing out of place on the main floor. It was only the basement that was a concern at the moment. But my concern was real. My anxiety high, getting higher. There was no explanation for the music being on. Not a good one anyway. I couldn't imagine how it was anything but bad.

"Babe, come on back down here for a minute," I yelled back up to Diane, wanting to get her on the main floor of the house, which I knew was safe. Then I stepped slowly and surely down the basement stairs.

The music grew louder as I descended. Louder with each step down. Louder, the closer I came to the stereo, which was around the back of the room near the bar. I didn't recognize the tune—it wasn't any of the newer, alternative rock tunes the boys would play—rather, it was some sort of Latin rock tune. It had a slow, rhythmic beat that repeated over and over and over. I could feel my heartbeat belting out its own rhythm. My stomach was clenched. I expected a dagger to my ribs or a bullet to my gut at any second.

As the room below came in to view, I slowly leveled the Stoeger and moved it from right to left and back again as I continued down one step at a time. At the base of the stairs, I turned right, stepping through my work out area as I headed toward the bar. The treadmill, weight bench, and dumb bells looked lonely and untouched. The beat continued on and on and on as I walked through the weight room and in to the playroom.

"What chew doing, mang?"

Roberto yelled it out over the music, as he stood behind the bar with a big grin on his face and one of my Stoegers in his hands, its barrel aimed directly at me. We were ten feet apart, pointing guns at each other. My shotgun was leveled right at him. I instinctively pulled the trigger.

Nothing happened.

"Your safety is still on, my man," Roberto yelled out, now in perfect English.

"But mine isn't," he continued. "Before I blow a hole in your chest with this nice new shotgun of yours, slowly put down the one you're holding."

How could this happen? How could I get trapped like this in my own house?

"Fuck!" Was all I could say.

"Fucked is more like it, Dan, my man." The words came out slowly, one by one, enunciated perfectly.

"Put the gun down," the words came slowly, one at a time, but grew in force and volume.

I hadn't spent enough time with the Stoeger to know exactly where the safety was, and the least bit of fumbling movement would result in him pulling the trigger on one of my own shotguns, sending me sprawling. His grip was steady and practiced. There would be no hesitation if I so much as wiggled a finger. There was no way he'd miss me at this range.

Not doing what he said would mean instant death. With me dead and no chance of getting his hands on the money, Roberto would satisfy his urge for revenge with a more brutal exchange. He'd kill Diane—maybe letting his men have their way with her first—then kill the boys when they came home from school. He'd finish them off one by one in whatever horrible fashion he desired. Slowly. Then he would burn the house down. I had to stay alive and keep looking for some sort of advantage so that I could save them. Save them all, regardless of what happened to me. I didn't know how that was possible, but I had no choice. I slowly bent down and put the shotgun on the floor.

The music stopped suddenly. It was only then that I noticed another man, much younger than Roberto. He sat on a chair ten feet to my right. He held the remote for the TV and stereo in one hand, and a pistol, pointed at me, in the other.

"Good boy," said Roberto, smiling towards Domingo, but the words were meant for me.

"Now, let's go upstairs to the kitchen so we can all sit around and have ourselves a little talk."

Just then, Diane let out a horrible scream from two floors up. My heart went from racing to pounding out of control.

"Your men better not hurt her!"

"Shut up, Dan," he said dismissively. "It's up to you what happens to your wife. Get it?"

He really wasn't asking a question. He motioned with his shotgun toward the stairs. Domingo, who had taken my Stoeger from me, walked up first, looking back down toward me as he climbed.

"Now get your ass up those stairs without trying anything stupid."

Diane had walked up the stairs to the second floor and gone first to Chris's room, then to Dave's. She had stacked clothes on each of their beds earlier. Now, she dragged their suitcases out of their closets, tossed them on their beds and packed them. Finished with everything but their hoodies and toiletries, which they could pack last in the morning, she walked satisfied to the master bedroom to finish up her own pack job. Getting this all out of the way now would give them all some quality family time tonight—something she desperately wanted and needed before the unknown craziness Roberto's visit would create.

As she walked through the master bedroom into the bath area, she imagined she saw a shadow or some sort of movement ahead of her, but that was impossible, she told herself calmly. No one was in the house except the two of us.

Which is why the sight of Victor sitting on the edge of the bathtub shocked her so.

She was face to face with this stranger, a sturdy, clean cut Hispanic who was calmly pointing a pistol at her, expressionless.

She let out a scream.

"Who are you? What do you want?"

Her body had jumped spasmodically as she whipped around to confront this man. So consumed with fear and terror, it was all she could do to utter the words.

"What?" She exhaled the word with despair and frustration, knowing instinctively this man worked for her husband's mortal enemy. It didn't matter who exactly he was. He was here to do whatever Roberto wanted him to do. And that no doubt included murdering her. No more words escaped her lips. Her body was frozen in place with fear.

Still expressionless, Victor stood up. After a couple of seconds that seemed like minutes, he spoke.

"Let's walk downstairs."

His voice and tone were calm and cool—the opposite of hers.

"What do you want?" She asked as she began to slowly walk toward the stairs, somehow finding the strength to both move and speak.

"It's not what I want, it's what Roberto wants."

Of course. Diane's head immediately was awash in a storm of thoughts. How many other men with guns were in her home? Was Roberto here, too? Did he even want the money or was he just here to avenge his brothers? Was Dan already dead in the basement?

"Ma'am?" Victor said sternly but politely.

Diane needed to get her head around some options. "Roberto is evil," is what Dan had told her. And the fact one of his men now had a gun pointed at her in her own bathroom certainly brought that sad fact home hard.

"Ma'am," Victor said loudly and much more forcefully.

"What?" She snapped, coming out of her haze, staring directly at the gun barrel and the man pointing it at her.

"Please, slowly walk down the stairs."

With guns still pointing to our backs, Diane and I ended up in the family room at exactly the same moment.

"Well, this isn't exactly how I had planned on spending the afternoon together." I said with a smile, hoping to both calm Diane and show Roberto I wasn't about to lose my shit.

Roberto was unimpressed and had his own idea of how to set the tone. He stepped in toward Diane, and still holding the shotgun in his right hand—which was leveled at me—draped his left arm over her shoulder and held her next to him.

"Don't we make a cute couple, Dan?"

191

I didn't say a word. I was still trying to maintain my smile, acting as if nothing he could do, would faze me. It was the wrong tact to take.

Roberto was now holding her close and began fondling her left ear. Diane looked to me as if she couldn't be any more uncomfortable, but Roberto would prove me wrong.

"You think this whole thing is funny or something?" He directed this question to me, head tilted quizzically, as he brought his left hand down in a sudden, jerking motion, pulling Diane's earring clean through her lobe and out, ripping through her flesh and sending blood streaming down her neck and shoulder.

Diane shrieked.

It was the kind of quick, unexpected, violent action Roberto was known for—a bold, spur of the moment decision designed to focus attention and get the upper hand—and as usual, it worked like a charm.

Diane's expression changed from terror, to pain, to shock in an instant. Her shriek seemed delayed from the violent action, but it was no less horrifying to hear. She flinched, screamed in pain and brought her hand up to her ear all in one, fluid, awful movement.

"NO!" I yelled with all my might as I took one step forward, only to have Victor, who was standing beside me, bring the butt of his Glock down on top of my head. In an instant, I was sprawled on my family room carpet, barely conscious. The room spun and shrunk as the edge of my vision blacked out.

Diane, whose scream had morphed seamlessly into a

continual sob, was being held upright by Roberto with one hand, while he waved the shotgun—my shotgun—around with his other hand, all the time yelling a stream of words I was having a hard time understanding. My head hurt badly. My thoughts were scrambled; vision fuzzy and my hearing didn't seem to be working.

I couldn't make out what Roberto was saying, even though he now stood inches from my face, yelling and waving his arms. Spit formed a string connecting his top and lower lips and droplets of it caught the hot wind of his outraged breath and flew into my face. Still, I couldn't understand any of it, I guess, because of that damn thunderbolt to my head Victor had laid on me—but then again, maybe it had something to do with the fact that Roberto… was speaking… in Spanish.

Even my scrambled brain knew that was not a good sign. I needed to get my shit together and slow the pace of this confrontation down—to get things calmer again and get Roberto interested in keeping us alive, rather than killing us.

"Roberto," I said over Diane's pained sobs, barely able to maintain my clarity as I spoke.

"Please don't hurt my wife."

The words came slowly but clearly. One at a time.

"Why not?" he asked, his head, still in that cocked, quizzical look that appeared more animal and primal than human and civilized.

At least he was speaking in English again, which meant his brain was engaged.

"Why shouldn't I hurt your wife?"

Diane and I made eye contact.

"Maybe I should just kill her now?" he continued, as he brought the shotgun up to the side of her head.

Our eyes still locked, I hadn't experienced a look as powerful since Julie and I stared into each other's eyes as we stepped onto that elevator in Denver all those years ago. Roberto had been there that day too. I hoped this day would end nothing like that one.

But unlike that event, which I didn't see coming and had no control over, I had a chance here to sway the outcome. This didn't have to end in horrible, violent tragedy.

As long as I was smart, cool, and focused.

"I have your money, Roberto," I said, now bringing my eyes to his.

"Yes, I know you do, my friend," he said nodding his head. There had been no hesitation in his response. The look on his face was more mocking smirk than angry scowl.

"You've had it all these years." His hold on Diane remained aggressive and threatening.

I ignored his uncaring sarcasm and kept pushing forward.

"If you pull that trigger, you will never see it. Not a penny of it. I won't care what you do to me after you shoot her. It won't matter. I won't change my mind. I'd burn the cash before giving it to you."

He began to slowly lower the shotgun with his right hand as he released his grip on Diane and brought his left hand across her back.

"Hmm," was the only sound he made as he nodded his head and pursed his lips. Maybe I had struck a nerve?

Diane was sobbing softly, still in shock, wondering if her

life would end in a violent flash and no doubt trying to figure out where I was going with this.

If only I knew.

"Maybe I have this all wrong, my friend." It seemed like a thoughtful response.

And maybe I finally had a beachhead from which to start some sort of meaningful negotiation.

"Maybe I should be injuring you and letting your lovely bride watch, hmm?"

OK, maybe not, but I had to keep pushing.

"Or maybe I should kill her now, right in front of you. That would set the right tone for how you should behave and what you should expect of me when your two young boys return home from school?"

"Whatever, Roberto."

"I have many cards to play, Dan. You have none."

I ignored his threat; let it bounce off me even though I knew that in Roberto's sick, twisted brain, this was a very tenable option. I kept going.

"I am prepared to give you your money. All of it, as you asked. Ten million dollars. In return, we all walk away and put that awful chapter of our lives behind us forever."

"You really think it's as easy as all that?"

There was no anger—no emotion at all in his voice. I couldn't yet tell if this was a good thing or not.

"Yes, Roberto. I do. I've got it all secured in an offshore account that only you can access, tax free."

"That's too bad." He cut me off as if he stopped listening after I said "yes".

"Let me get this straight," he crinkled up his face and brought his hand to his chin as if he were actually considering the terms, "So you have a full grasp of the situation."

"I let you give me MY money," his voice started to rise as he said "my" and pointed at me.

And with that gesture, I knew in my heart that I didn't have a chance to steer the outcome of this day. My future, my wife's future, and my children's future were out of my control and in the hands of an irrational madman with vengeance on his mind.

"And maybe, I let you go free." His voice still carried more than a hint of danger.

"Or maybe not."

I was half convinced he was about to point the gun at me, pull the trigger and end it all. But he didn't. He had another surprise up his sleeve.

"How about instead of killing anyone right now, I just have a little fun?"

And with that, he brought his hand up to Diane's right ear and with one quick motion, gave a quick, violent tug. There was an actual popping noise this time, almost like someone snapping their fingers, as he yanked Diane's other earring down and through her earlobe.

Diane screamed, more loudly this time.

Roberto's action had surprised her. In turn, she surprised everyone in the room by instinctively backhanding her right hand up and around behind her—catching Roberto square in the nose. There was another popping noise as one of the bones in Roberto's nose gave way. That wasn't going to be a good thing for any of us. Lucky for me, he wasn't pointing the shotgun in my direction.

Domingo wasn't as fortunate.

Roberto's trigger finger pulled as instinctively as Diane's backhand shot out. The blast caught Domingo dead center in his chest, lifting him up and back, catapulting him through the air and into the wall behind me. The shotgun blast likely killed him instantly, blowing a quarter size hole in his heart. Domingo held firmly onto the Glock until his already dead body slammed into the wall, forcing the gun free and sending it skidding across the floor directly next to my foot.

It was my turn to act instinctively. Even though the shocking violence-laced actions of the previous ten seconds should have frozen me in place, I bent quickly, picking up the Glock. I stood up and pointed the gun at Roberto, fully prepared to shoot him dead. But this wasn't Roberto's first throw down. While only seconds had passed since he pulled the earring out and accidentally shot Domingo, he was ready and calm, standing there facing me with a handful of Diane's hair in one hand and his shotgun, warm and lightly smoking, in the other—pressed firmly against my wife's head.

"This is where you slowly put that gun down on the floor and kick it over to me," he said, loud enough to be heard over the ringing in my ears from the thunderous shotgun blast going off in such close quarters.

Diane had a wide-eyed look of terror on her face. Tears were streaming down her cheeks, mixing with the blood from the fresh wounds to her ears. Her body heaved up and down with big, gulping sobs.

"Otherwise, your wife's face will look just like Julie's. You remember that look, don't you?"

He was speaking slowly and calmly but his eyes had a wide, crazed look that appeared to say, *Fuck it, I don't care what happens.*

And perhaps most incredibly, Roberto mimicked a scrunched-up mocking face at me, the same look on Julie's face in her final repose.

It was a look that said, *I'm fucking crazy, so don't even try and gain the upper hand here because even I don't know what I might do next.*

"And the money you owe me? Meh…" He made a guttural noise as if to say he could care less. And if there were any doubt, he confirmed it immediately.

"I don't need the money you owe me, Dan. This really isn't about that."

He shrugged, continuing, "Blowing your wife's head off in front of you was always a possibility in my mind. Perhaps an even better outcome than getting my hands on that money."

He tugged at Diane's hair, jerking her head as he did, "Sorry darling."

She was terrified. Wide-eyed with tears streaming down her face, she looked helpless and hopeless.

Back at me now, Roberto said, "You have to admit, it's not a bad way to get my vengeance."

He turned back toward Diane and looked her in the eyes

as he talked of killing her. Her own eyes grew wider and wider. The tears were coming in a steady stream now and the sobs were joined by body trembles.

"That's why, of the three of us, I'm the only one that possibility doesn't bother."

He just let that hang there, looked over at Victor, who stood behind me, staring at Domingo with concern. Victor had his own shotgun pointed calmly at me for insurance. I'd forgotten he was even in the room. Glancing over at Domingo must have snapped Roberto back to some sort of reality.

I put the Glock down slowly and kicked it over to Roberto as he had asked. He picked it up, smiling, and tucked it in his waist.

"Good boy. Now go see if Domingo has a pulse and get your wife a towel for those nasty cuts on her ears."

Chapter 22

My heart was pounding out of my chest with nervous anxiety, probably running up to or over 120 beats per minute as I stood there. Domingo had no pulse. He was dead, just as we all thought he would be, lying there on my floor in a big pool of sticky red blood with a hole in his chest.

Diane was sitting in a chair, looking like Princess Leia from Star Wars with buns on either side of her head. But instead of a well-quaffed, other-world hairdo, she wore wads of toilet paper duct taped around her ear lobes. Victor had found the tape and silently thrown it and a roll of toilet paper to her from the bathroom while I had checked on Domingo. The improvised bandage she managed to concoct didn't look stylish, but it got the job done and stemmed the bleeding.

"Tsk, tsk, tsk," the irritating noises were part scold and part insult and rolled off Roberto's tongue in a staccato, snapping beat.

"What are we going to do now, my friend?" the words slipped off Roberto's tongue mockingly, keeping that same beat.

I was speechless. I had no words and I had no plan.

"I mean, here you go again, killing one of my family."

The words were delivered in Roberto's classic overly dramatic, over the top performance speak. This was part of the show—both for me and Diane—and for him and his men. It was designed to set a tone. I'd seen him use the technique plenty of times over that lost summer many years ago. Sometimes it didn't lead anywhere—he was simply amusing himself. Other times it led to beatings, bloodletting, or a trip in the Land Rover to a final resting place. It was too soon to tell which this was. If it was my swan song, I'm sure Roberto had it planned out exactly.

He was using the shotgun as a pointer, aiming it in my general direction as I knelt next to Domingo's lifeless body.

"This is as good a time as any, Dan, to get it all out in the open, don't you think?"

As quickly as his tone had gone all dramatic, it now went all serious and believable. I honestly had no idea what he was referring to or where he was headed.

"Get what all out in the open?" I managed to ask.

My words came out softly, without thought, expression or emotion. I was physically spent and out of options.

"What happened in that hotel room."

His words came out flat and emotionless, matching my own in tone. But he wasn't spent. Roberto was just getting going.

I let out a deep exhale and stood up slowly. I had blood splatter on the back of my shirt, and blood stains on my shoes and pants. I looked down at my hands, which were covered in Domingo's blood. My mind began to swirl in painful memories and visions.

Seemingly reading my mind, Roberto gave me a push into the past, "Just like that day in Denver, you have blood on your hands again today, Dan."

Roberto's words brought the emotions of that day—that horrible, bloody, violent day so many years ago—flooding back from the deep recesses of my being where I had kept them locked away and all but forgotten about. But now, in an instant, they came flooding back and came pouring out and it was overwhelming.

"Fuck you, Roberto!" I blurted it out without thinking, looking him in the eye. I went from zero to sixty, the raw emotions unchecked as they rushed up and out of my brain.

"Ah, you feel it."

He was smiling. As if my torment brought him some sort of perverse joy.

"The memory is real. It is awful, no?" Again with a Cuban accent, out of the blue, just for dramatic effect.

"What happened that day is all on you, Roberto," I shouted, but he continued on as if I hadn't spoken.

"Is that what you told yourself all those years in order to live with it? To live with beautiful Julie's death? The death of my brothers?"

Roberto's insanity was laid naked before me. He had twisted not just what happened, but the blame for what had happened—the violence, blood and murders—and worked it all into something he could hang on me. He'd manipulated his guilt over the years—his greed—into hatred and it had driven him to this, a place where he could relieve himself of his own pain by punishing me.

"And you blame ME for that? Really? Is that what you told yourself, Roberto? Is that how YOU were able to live with the deaths of your brothers all those years?"

Spittle flew from my lips as I released my own anger, born from a frustration I had carried for decades, buried deep and unreachable. Yes, a part of it was guilt and anger for my own greed and stupidity and for Julie's terrible murder. A part of me had never come to terms with the awful suddenness with which she had disappeared. She'd been vaporized from my life and the world. Painted with history's brush as some sort of drug dealing sexy sidekick.

For my part, I was complicit with how she met her end that day, and I had tried hard to come to terms with my involvement and responsibility in that. I could have ended our drug mule business at any point—or better yet—never even begun it. I had many potential paths that didn't take us to that Denver hotel room, but I'd failed to take any of them. But in the end, it was Roberto's decision to attack. He and his brothers ignited that firestorm and it was a bullet from one of his own brother's guns that blew a hole in Julie's head and extinguished her life.

But there was more—I had an angst built up inside that had been unable to be spoken for. Born from years of hiding, adapting, changing who I was—my very identity—to hide from and avoid the past. That was a pain and isolation I'd not shared with anyone, not even myself. And now, it was unleashed.

"It was your greed, your plan, and your bullets that killed everyone in that room you fucking crazy, murdering egomaniac. You killed Julie and YOU killed your brothers. It was you. All YOU! You might as well have pulled the trigger yourself, you fucking lunatic."

Roberto closed the five feet between us in an instant with two big steps, turned the shotgun around and leveled its butt into my stomach with all his might. The blunt force knocked all the air out of my lungs and doubled me over.

I could hear his heavy breathing while he stood over me as I struggled to find my own breath. I half expected another blow from the shotgun butt against my skull, but it didn't come. As I struggled to breathe, I could hear he was still talking—only now he was speaking to Diane.

"You believe this shit?" The words, the immediate threat, and the shotgun were all pointed at her.

"This man kept his deepest, darkest secret from you until it leapt from the shadows and into your life. Only then did he reveal it to you. Why? Because he had no choice. He was caught in a lie, like a little boy with a secret he was ashamed of and afraid to tell you. You! His wife!" He paused for effect.

"His soul mate."

The last two words dripped slowly off his tongue. "Soul. Mate."

He let them hang in the air for a few seconds before continuing.

"And he would never have told you. Not ever."

He looked back at me now and repeated it mockingly.

"Soul mate."

Again, he paused, and then turned back to Diane.

"He would have kept it from you until he was dead and buried. He only told you because he was forced to. Caught in a lie and facing exposure, humiliation, and death—I forced him to tell you. To grow up. To be a man."

He leaned in and whispered to her, "You should thank me."

Diane said nothing. Her ears were ringing and crusted with drying blood, and her mind was scrambled from the events of the past few minutes. She was in shock—and the shocks seemed to have no end in sight. Surprised by armed men in her home, assaulted not once, but twice, and then witnessing a man shot to death just feet from her. This was too much to get her mind around. Now this crazy man was waving a shotgun at her and Dan—and by the looks of it, he was going to kill them both once he was done ranting.

"I let him into my life and trusted him. Him and his girlfriend."

Roberto kept on going. He would not be stopped.

"Julie."

The name came out with a sort of disgust that he must have hoped Diane also felt when she heard it. But she was too numb to feel or register anything.

He bent down to her, looked her in the eyes, and then leaned in again.

"Julie," he whispered it with that same disdain.

This was a part of why he came here. A big part. It wasn't just the revenge, it was to re-write history. Sure, he was here to dish out torment, pain, and fear, but he wanted more. He needed more. He wanted to shame and humiliate me in front of my wife.

He would absolve himself of the pain and guilt that he'd carried for decades by washing his hands of it and instead, paint me as a plotting villain who'd gotten in his way, botched his own plan from working and caused the deaths of his brothers. And then, adding insult to injury, he would pronounce for all to hear that I'd turned traitor and stolen his money and drugs. He wasn't to blame. He was a victim.

Sure he'd come here for his money, and to kill me, whether I gave it to him or not. He needed this confrontation—it was cathartic remedy for what ailed him—as much as he needed his blood revenge.

It was all good. In Roberto's world, the best possible outcome would be to get me to give him the millions of dollars he felt was owed to him, and to consummate that exchange with my humiliation and death.

The message was for me, but he continued to deliver it by talking to me through Diane.

"Dan and his girl, Julie."

He'd stood up and taken a step back, walking around so he could look directly into Diane's eyes as he spoke.

"They were real lovebirds, Diane. Soul mates, I think is how they described themselves to me and my brothers. Isn't that so Dan?"

I didn't remember ever talking to Roberto or his brothers about my personal life or my relationship with Julie, but there was no time to defend myself and no stopping him. Roberto kept up his verbal assault.

"Soul mates, yeah," he nodded his head and smiled at me before turning back to Diane and continuing.

"Love birds and soul mates. Until he got her killed."

He leaned back in and cocked his head, so his lips were near her ear, but his head was turned around, so his eyes were on me.

"And now, he's going to get YOU killed."

He walked around behind Diane, stopping as he faced me. The deadly Stoeger was cradled gently in front of him. He leveled it at the back of her head and tapped the barrel on her shoulder. Diane winced.

"I want my money, Dan."

"I have it. That's not a problem. I have it all."

"Good. And I want an apology. And not necessarily by the way, in that order."

There was silence. Victor repositioned himself directly behind me in a chair over by the TV. He was settling in for what he was sure was the dramatic conclusion to today's adventure. His arm rested on the arm of the chair, Glock firmly gripped, pointing at my back.

For the second time, I'd forgotten he was even in the room. Ten seconds passed.

"I'm sorry."

The silence lasted longer than 30 seconds this time.

Roberto smiled, almost kind of chuckled as if he were let in on a not so funny joke.

"Yeah, that's not quite the apology I had in mind, Dan."

Roberto tapped the Stoeger on Diane's shoulder again, looking at me and smirking, as if to say, *Give me a good apology with lots of emotion or the girl gets it.*

Diane's reaction was less of a wince and more of a scowl. She hadn't spoken in quite some time and both Roberto and Dan were thinking separately to themselves that she was probably at wit's end. Frazzled, in shock, emotionally unstable, and raw; Roberto was taking advantage and picking at her like she was a delicate scab.

But in truth, neither had a clue as to the emotions that had run through, taken over and defined her this past hour. She was an exposed electrical wire—frayed and dangerous. She could pop, snap, explode, or pass out from the sheer physical and emotional strain at any moment. Her mind no longer felt like her own.

In Diane's current world, Roberto's words had gone from being the only things she was connected to, to being faint, abstract distractions. His threats had consumed her mind, but she ran with them so far, that she ran away from the real world, too. She had visions playing out—picturing her and Dan tortured near death, being forced to watch their boys shot or stabbed or mutilated or raped, then murdered in front of them.

While the words were real but faint and seemed to waft over her as if they were part of some silent evil fog rolling in from the sea; she felt his actions much more sharply and acutely.

Each whisper brought his breath to her ear and face, birthing revulsion deep inside her. Each tap of the Stoeger on her shoulder felt like an electrical shock that ran through her entire body with white hot pain.

"Do you want to live, Diane?"

He might have said it more than once, but once was all that she heard and all that registered. He was in front of her now, bending down, face to face, mere inches apart.

She nodded slowly while looking him square in the eyes.

"And your two handsome, young boys, do you want them to live too?"

His words seemed without life. They were said slightly above a whisper in a deadpan, emotionless voice that had no rhythm or feeling.

Diane nodded again. Expressionless but now laser focused, looking him in the eye as she nodded. Mentioning her boys had evaporated the fog that had enshrouded her.

"Yes, of course you do. You're a good mother. But this man before us…"

Roberto tapped her again with the Stoeger—this time, just under her chin. If he pulled the trigger, her head would come off clean and roll around the floor while her life and blood shot out of her neck.

That visual lasted a fleeting second or two. Her entire body had tensed and jolted with a violent jerk as the now cool, steel touched her feverish skin.

"This man," Roberto continued. "He's a liar, a little boy afraid of the truth. Afraid of the past. He's put you and your lovely boys in harm's way, Diane."

He was still standing close in front of her, sort of bent from the waist so that his head was about the same level as hers, while she sat.

"Maybe I should just take his money, kill him, and let you and the boys go?"

Roberto stood and began to slowly pace back and forth a couple of feet in front of Diane. One hand made odd, chopping movements while the other, carrying the Stoeger, waived back and forth in a slow, crazy arc from left to right—then back again.

"Or maybe I should just stick to the plan."

Roberto had stopped dead center in front of Diane, bending down so their eyes were locked and the space between their faces was less than a foot.

"The Plan, in case you're curious, Diane, is to take your husband's money. All of it. Not just what he has set aside for me, but all of it. My people have already figured out how to access it. All of it."

Now he turned and looked to me.

"My people," he spoke softly, but his pride was apparent.

"I only have to call them, and they'll move your money, Dan. ALL your money, to my accounts."

He laughed that crazy, Roberto-insane laugh, and threw his head back a little.

"I'll take all your money, Dan. How's that feel?"

I stood motionless and expressionless while he laughed at me and mocked me.

"I'll do it over the phone with my people in Miami. We'll put them on speaker—so you can hear it all go down and have a full appreciation for it—so you can fully understand that all you had, you had because of me."

He smiled, and then continued.

"And how all you have now, will be taken by me. What you have will be nothing. It will all be gone. It will all be mine."

He nodded his head softly a couple of times and smiled, obviously very happy with himself and how things were turning out.

"That's the plan, Dan. Not all of it mind you, but most of it. Do you want to hear the rest, hmm?"

He turned to Diane.

"How about you, sweet Diane? Do you want to hear the rest of The Plan?"

He paused, looked at me smiling, then back to her and continued.

"Oh, I think you do."

He stepped in even closer to Diane now, leaning down, not wanting her to miss any of what he was about to say. He spoke louder now, so that neither one of us would have any trouble hearing him. No trouble understanding him.

"Once we have all my money back—you know, your money—I'm going to turn my attention to you."

He tapped her under the chin with the shotgun again, sending another electric bolt of hot hatred through her. Her body tensed, jerked, and lifted, just barely, off the chair, then settled back in. Her eyes were wide, staring straight into Roberto's.

"I'm going to have my way with you. Nothing gentle, I don't like gentle. I like rough. Real rough. You might not like it, Diane. It will rip at you and hurt you. But it's not about you; it's about me, me and your husband. I'll make him watch the entire time. Maybe I'll even peel off his eyelids, so he'll be forced to watch."

He looked back at me, smiling. Diane was still staring

into his face, not moving but wound as tight as a person could be.

"Then, when I'm done, Victor back there, he's going to have his way with you. And Victor likes it rough, too. I'm not going to lie, Diane. You're going to like Victor even less than me. But it's OK, because when we're both done with you, your part in this little scene is over. I'm going to take this shotgun and blow your pretty little face off, right in front of Dan."

"Fuck you, Roberto!" It was all I could muster.

"No Dan, Fuck Diane!"

He threw his head back and laughed a loud, sickening laugh.

"But as they say on the TV game shows, wait, there's more!"

He laughed even louder. Diane again began trembling and shaking ever so slightly. Not from fear or terror, but rather, from hatred.

"Victor and I will have Dan tied up nice and tight and gagged, so the boys don't hear him screaming in agony when they come home from school."

I lurched forward but Victor hit me hard across the back of my neck with the butt of his Glock, which sent me straight back down in my chair, nearly blacking out. Roberto kept on talking as if nothing happened.

"We'll bring them in here, so they can see their dad tied up and crying. And see you, dear Diane, naked and spread eagled and dead on the floor, your face blown clean off. And as they raise their young voices into a tearful scream, I'll shoot them both dead, in front of Dan, so he has those sweet, sweet memories to live with for the rest of his life."

Roberto leaned in close—again almost face to face—and tapped Diane one last time under the chin with the business end of the double barrel Stoeger. His intent was to torture me as much as Diane. But what happened next surprised everyone in the room and was definitely not part of The Plan.

Chapter 23

The words had stripped her nerves raw. The Stoeger's tap on her chin provided the spark that sent one more electrical current—more of a surge—through her entire body. The result was as if a switch had been thrown, triggering an explosion of neurons firing as one. It was like nothing she had ever experienced before and something over which she had absolutely no control. The jolt caused her to stand straight up, in an instant. Her forehead cracked into Roberto's, forcing him to take a stumbling backward step, slack-jawed and starry-eyed. One arm came up as they connected, knocking into the Stoeger, pointing it away from her. Her other arm moved with purpose as Roberto fell back, grabbing the Glock out of his waist band. In a blind rage, she brought it up quickly, pointing it straight at his chest at point blank range.

Roberto had only a second to react, but years of experience eliminated the need for thinking to force a physical reaction. As Diane freed the Glock from his waistband, instinct took over. He shifted to the side as he fell backward, and Diane brought the Glock up, pointed it and fired. His nimble move saved the day for him, and he was able to deflect the Glock with his free hand just enough so that it moved away from his chest before discharging in a thunderously loud roar.

Roberto's good fortune was my bad luck. The bullet ripped through the air millimeters from his body and struck me, ripping into my flesh at the top of my shoulder, tearing through the bottom of my clavicle. The impact picked me up off my feet and knocked me to the floor, stunned and silent. The bullet didn't break through the clavicle clean, but rather deflected down from the bone, cracking it, and then sailing clear through me and out my back. As bad as it was for me, it was worse for Victor. The deflection was just enough to redirect it straight toward his head. He had no time to react, and caught the projectile straight in his wide open, shocked mouth as he sat in the chair behind me. The bullet shredded off his jaw and tore a hole through the back of his head, killing him instantly. His now nearly headless body tumbled to the floor, blood spilling out from him like it came from an open faucet.

The surprising, swift, unexpected death—murder— should have come as a shock to Dan and Diane's normal suburban sensibilities, but it didn't. The numbing speed and finality froze the moment and their emotions. In the split second that followed, Diane looked at Victor, then at me, more concerned with my fresh injury, than the lifeless, bloody body on our increasingly stained basement floor.

Roberto stopped his backward stumble with a stiff-legged brace and stepped forward. He'd lost control of the attack and if he didn't regain the upper hand immediately, with firmness and authority, all could be lost.

He turned quickly, on his toes now and ready to bring the shotgun up and fire immediately. But the girl had a new-found spunk and animalistic survival instinct. She beat him to the draw. As he looked up, he was staring down the barrel of the handgun she held at eye level. Without the slightest quiver, Diane pointed it squarely at his face.

"Drop that shotgun, fucker."

He stared at her in disbelief—at her swiftness, daring, and ultimately, her amazing restraint. He admired the calm, cool professionalism—it was the stuff trained killers brought to situations like this one and it wasn't what Roberto was expecting from this blonde, pampered housewife and mother.

"Put. That. Down," Diane said, now in a barely audible, exasperated voice. "Now."

Roberto looked at her, his shotgun still by his side, pointing down uselessly; surprised she hadn't already pulled the trigger.

"I will," he said, standing motionless.

There was no fear on his face. Instead, he was oddly calm. A slight smile seemed to cross his lips.

"But before you pull the trigger and kill me, something which you have every right to do, I'd ask you to stop and look around."

"Why," Diane said with disgust, clearly intending to kill him as soon as he put the shotgun down, sending him straight to the eternal torment she believed he so richly deserved. Her finger ached to pull the trigger.

"Because my third man, Fortunato, is standing just behind you, holding a gun to the head of one of your sons."

Chapter 24

"I will not turn around," she shouted out, her voice no longer quiet.

"Unless and until I shoot you first," she finished the statement with both disgust and resolve.

"Then you will kill me—and you will kill your child," Roberto said with a long pause and a slight nod toward the door leading from the basement to the yard.

"A bullet from your gun to my heart and a bullet from my man's gun to your son's head. A life for a life. Very biblical. Very final. Very unfortunate."

Once the confrontation had begun, Roberto had forgotten all about Fortunato. He'd been a last-minute addition to the expedition to Pittsburgh and he'd assigned him all the lowest level tasks a novice apprentice would be expected to fulfill. He'd forgotten he'd left him at the Eat n' Park parking lot watching me and Diane but now was grateful for the unexpected break. Grateful he'd made the last-minute decision to bring three men, not two. Grateful that he'd left Fortunato in place at the restaurant parking lot. Grateful that Fortunato had the good sense to come back to this house when the lines of communication had gone silent, and above all, he was grateful that Fortunato had the smarts to grab the kid when Chris was letting himself in the garage, having just been dropped off by the school bus up the road. That piece of luck was a game changer and had given Fortunato access to the house and a hostage, and ultimately, had saved Roberto's life, which was about to be extinguished after all these years of drug dealing and violence, by an enraged, homicidal housewife. His apprentice was due a raise when they got back to Miami.

"It seems primitive, but it is a very equal form of justice—an eye for an eye. Biblical, yes, but still effective."

Roberto continued, staring straight into her eyes.

"The life of a killer for that of a son. It may not have the same panache as say, the story of Cain and Abel, but I think once you look behind you, it'll have more impact on you and you'll understand where I'm coming from."

Their eyes still locked, intense and not blinking. He feared she would still just pull the trigger, not believing a word he was saying. He plowed ahead.

"Believe it or not, I've been in your shoes, Diane. My back against the wall, facing an evil stranger who I was convinced wanted me dead, and feeling likc I was out of options. But it's always wiser to take a moment to consider every step, every action, every consequence. Once you pull that trigger, there will be no turning back. There'll be no undoing what you will have finished—and started."

Roberto had blurted out what appeared to be a last second Hail Mary. I thought it was a bluff too—a good one—and was surprised Diane didn't just pull the trigger in the middle of his rant. Why wouldn't this be a bluff? It would be just like him—a last-ditch desperate deception meant to deceive Diane and make her turn her attention away for even a split second—just long enough so that Roberto could blast her into oblivion.

I was shot and injured, bleeding, but not broken and dying. While their eyes remained locked, I took the briefest of moments to look around and see for myself if there was any truth to Roberto's plea. And when I did, my eyes told an awful, different story from what my heart had hoped. I spoke up immediately.

"Diane," I said firmly and loudly, and hopefully with enough forceful emotion to stop her finger from squeezing the trigger. "He's not lying. His man has Chris. Do as he says. Put the gun down."

The words were delivered with the last ounce of calm sanity I had left in me. It was my own Hail Mary pass. My son's life depended on it.

Still holding the handgun high and aimed squarely at Roberto's face, my words had sown the seeds of doubt in her resolute mind. Diane slowly turned her head around.

She stood transfixed for what seemed like an eternity but was probably more like a minute. No one else moved or said a word. Silently, she slowly lowered the gun, still gazing out into the yard at her son, standing there with a gun to his head and a strange, terrified look on his face. Her once steady hand now quivered. Where there was a glimmer of hope, now only despair again filled her heart. The shaking in her hand spread across her body and her chest heaved in and out in a big, resentful sigh as she began to sob.

"That a girl, Diane," said Roberto, quickly beginning to fill again with confidence and bravado.

"A wise choice. Really, your only choice."

He moved quickly to close the gap between them and took her hand, still holding the gun but now pointing downward and shaking. He took it in both his hands and relieved her of the gun and the last sense of hope remaining inside her.

He held it in his hand for a moment, gazing at it as if he were expecting it to tell him what to do with it. It must have whispered something only Roberto could hear, because after a bit, he walked over to me and hit me hard on my head with it, replacing my anguish and pain with blackness.

Chapter 25

I awoke to a world of throbbing pain. My head cleared slowly, from a dark fogginess through a blurry haze to a headache and the stark reality now before me. My shoulder throbbed with searing pain, hurting more with each heartbeat. I looked down and saw that the wound still oozed fresh blood. Was this through and through enough to finish me off, or would Roberto now have that pleasure?

Not that any of that mattered at the moment. I was in a chair in my basement facing Diane and Chris. They too, were in chairs facing me. Fortunato stood behind them. He held a shotgun leveled in his hands.

"Ah, time to rise and shine, eh Dan?"

Roberto stood behind me. His always taunting voice penetrating me like the hot lead of the bullet that struck me.

"Did you have a nice little nap, Danny boy?"

He tapped me on the back of my shoulder with his shotgun as he spoke the words. I winced in pain.

He stopped talking and just stood there and stared at me, seemingly at a loss for words. To the untrained eye, it would have appeared that the unexpected action of the past fifteen minutes was perhaps so crazy, so violent, so off the chains that even the violence prone and seasoned Roberto was now left speechless.

But I knew better. Roberto had been in situations like this before—in worse situations in fact. He wasn't frozen or speechless or incapable of reacting. He was calculating and cool. This was the end game he'd been playing toward and looking forward to. He'd been working with this or something like this in his mind all along. He'd come here for this eventuality and was prepared for it. He'd pushed and pushed, applying pressure until this final confrontation came into view, and now he would apply one last, awful pressure to me—directly, or through Diane or Chris.

Then he would kill us all. And that he would do with much fanfare and enjoyment.

I remembered this cold, calculating, silent look of his—I'd seen it on Roberto's face all those years ago, back when we were both much younger, and I was naïve and stupid. I knew it meant he was about to get down to business and get what he wanted—what he demanded. Then, he'd call it a day and kill whoever his target was, in cruel, methodical fashion, sending a message to all that he was larger than life and never to be trifled with. Ever.

Ultimately, the violent endings hardly ever really made sense to anyone but Roberto. Most of the time the situation ended with him getting what he wanted, but sometimes that didn't happen. Sometimes the target, the victim—for whatever reason—pride, stubbornness, stupidity, wouldn't tell or give him what he wanted. In those cases, he simply killed the people regardless. Back in the day, they would either vanish without a trace, or their bodies would show up in public as a message for others. No matter the outcome, Roberto seemed content. He was in charge and ultimately, that mattered most.

The point was, I was well aware I had mere seconds to make a move before Roberto set his plan in motion. If I failed, Diane, Chris, or I would die soon, followed by whoever else was still alive. And if I did nothing at all, I knew that in the moments ahead, one or all of us would likely be tortured and then killed anyway.

"I am growing tired of you people," Roberto said, as if on cue, confirming everything I'd just been thinking through.

"Tired of you, tired of your pathetic attempts at rescuing yourselves from this situation—for a debt you only owe me because of your own greed and stupidity."

He began to slowly wave the shotgun around as he spoke, swaying side to side as he worked his way across the room from behind me to alongside Diane and Chris. Fortunato stood slightly to the side of Diane, closer to me.

This was how Roberto would start working himself up. From what I remembered, it was something he needed to do to get in the right frame of mind. Maybe he simply liked this part of the process and the entire shit show wouldn't be as enjoyable to him without the prelude. Whatever the reason, this walk up to the full sprint was always step one and he never went full crazy without this slow, methodical starting point.

He'd talk himself some smack.

Pretty soon that gun would be resting on someone's shoulder or pointed at someone's head or heart. The smack talk would continue the entire time. He was working himself up into the frenzy he needed to pull the trigger. I didn't have much time.

"Maybe I should just shoot the kid in the leg or something?"

It was the first we'd heard from Fortunato, who was not only a disciple of Roberto's, but apparently, he was also a chip off the old block.

I was counting on having a few more minutes to plot my move, hoping I'd be able to stand slowly and maybe make a lunge at one of them and grab a gun. But that hope was beginning to look like a pipe dream.

With Fortunato engaged, and in the game, I needed to move before Roberto's words stopped and the action started. But even as I was running my options through my mind, it became clear there was no time to wait. I needed to move now.

But Fortunato made his move first, beating me to the punch. He sidestepped to a table and set the shotgun down, then pulled a handgun from his waistband. Taking one quick step toward Diane, he raised the gun and slammed the butt of it down into the top of her shoulder.

She'd been quiet for the last couple of minutes—she was probably still in shock—but the blunt force of the sturdy gun coming down hard on her shoulder sent a shockwave of pain through her.

Her scream was loud, authentic, and full of pain. The blow had come out of nowhere. She'd been numbed—having gone from a feeling of control when she'd had a loaded gun trained on Roberto—and deciding she would be justified in killing him—to where she was now, stripped of any advantage, sitting here next to her terrified son and across from her potentially fatally injured husband.

The blow had shaken her free from the pity and depression she felt and replaced it with sheer terror and pain. She instinctively pulled herself into a ball and brought her arms up around her head to protect herself from another blow.

"Mom!" Chris yelled, terrified, completely unprepared for what was happening. He had fallen into a world of terror and threat from one of comfortable complacency, and he had no idea how he had gotten here or where it was going to end. He'd seen enough movies to have a reasonable idea that this would not end well for him or his parents.

"There, there young man," Roberto said in a fake soothing voice as he put his free hand on the boy's shoulder, patting it with pretend paternal projections as he glanced over toward me. He wanted to make sure I was watching. Wanting to make sure I knew he was completely in control. That the fate of my family rested in his hands.

"We're all a little tense here. We just need your mom and you to sit tight where you are and for your dad to pay attention and do as he's told."

He turned fully toward me and contorted his face into a smile that hid his real intentions from no one.

"Do you think you can do that, Dan?"

His grin transformed into a smirk, which he shared with Fortunato, who he had now quickly turned his attention to.

The words and looks they enjoyed and shared were directed toward Chris and meant for me, but as they exchanged them and enjoyed their own little game, they ignored me. They were toying with us now and getting into it. With guns in their hands, neither of them were afraid of or paying particularly close attention to the rest of us. Our pain and suffering was their enjoyment. This lapse in attention wouldn't last.

"Yeah…" Fortunato blurted out with a gleeful smile.

They were pigs.

I leapt at Fortunato from where I was—just flat out leapt—in a total, unthinking, instantaneous movement that pushed my body through the air like a spear, flat out level with my arms outstretched before me and my feet and legs trailing behind. My thinking brain was no longer in control. My actions could be disastrous or successful, but no amount of reasoning would have approved them ahead of time or could have determined their outcome.

My fists slammed into Fortunato with the full weight of my propelled body, hitting him in his right arm. The impact forced him to squeeze the trigger of the handgun, which was positioned just behind Diane's head. The ear-splitting sound would leave her hearing impaired in her left ear for the remainder of her days, which thankfully, didn't come to an end in that moment.

Instead of ripping through her, Chris or me, the bullet

tore into Roberto. It struck him in his right forearm, shattering the bone before exiting and passing in and out his side and then lodging in a wall. The impact forced him to drop the shotgun he was about to bring down next to Chris's head. Instead of threatening him, it fell useless to the floor beside him.

Fortunato and I fell to the floor stunned.

Roberto lay motionless on the floor across from us.

Diane and Chris sat in chairs watching wide-eyed.

My world was engulfed in a firestorm of motion and violence. Bodies were flying in all directions and things were now happening fast and all at once. Too many things to fully comprehend, but one thing was certain—there would likely be no escape for any of us without the deaths of some of us.

This was a life and death battle for each one of us.

A fleeting, awful, fearful thought tore through my adrenaline-filled brain: The only other time I'd ever been in a situation quite like this, where there was so much life-threatening activity happening all around me, so quickly, so violently, was in that hotel room back in Denver all those years ago.

I wondered if Roberto was thinking of that day too. We'd both been there that fateful day and everything we'd done since had led us both to this room, facing the possibility of a similar, deadly outcome for one or both of us. Here we were again, each with bullet holes in us, once again in a similar all or nothing, life or death situation, both of us determined to survive.

Fortunato had fallen to the floor in a heap, and I clearly

still maintained some element of surprise over him. With my ears ringing from the gunshot, I vowed silently to myself that this day would end differently and pushed my aching, injured body up and punched him in the face with all my might, slamming his head back down into the floor.

He made a grunting, groaning, guttural noise and brought his hands to his face.

"What the fuck!" He mumbled, barely being heard.

What the fuck indeed. I punched him in the face again. Hard.

Fortunato had been caught totally off guard. He'd been cocksure he and his boss had this in hand. Cocky and sure he would walk out alive and richer for his efforts. Now he had the taste of his own blood in his mouth as it ran out his nose and down his chin and his fate was anything but a sure thing.

I pulled up off my elbows, my shoulder now screaming in pain. I ignored it and somehow managed to roll around his body. I grabbed him from behind, coming around and almost under him, locking my forearm securely around his throat. I grabbed my arm with my other hand, planted my feet on the floor, arched my back, and worked with all my might to choke the life out of him.

"Fucker!" he managed to exclaim as he exhaled, the fear now palpable as he realized his predicament.

Fortunato couldn't believe what was happening. A minute ago he had a gun in his hand and the fate of me and my family seemed securely in his and Roberto's hands. Now he had the metallic taste of fear rising up in his throat, mixing with his own blood. He'd been on the other end of this sort of situation and instinctively knew what could be coming, and he exploded in panic to avoid it.

Fortunato writhed, squirmed, groaned, and threw his arms and legs about violently. I didn't—I couldn't—release my grip. The only way to maintain the upper hand and stand any chance of getting out of here alive was to do this—this grisly, murderous thing—while Roberto was down, and to then deal with him one on one afterward.

Spit flew from Fortunato's mouth as he gurgled and groaned and fought with all his might against me. But I had the advantage of position and a grip I was unwilling to release. His body squirmed, wriggled, and fought back viciously, his hands trying to find a grip on me or gouge my eyes out. Anything to make me stop, but my grip around him only tightened. His breathing came harder in short, loud, ugly bursts as we struggled. His breaths made strange, awful noises. His feet began kicking wildly at the air. His eyes bulged outwards and darted around unfocused and afraid.

I was breathing loudly and hard. Big bursts of air came out my mouth like blasts from a steam engine as I struggled with all I had to not just maintain my stranglehold but to increase it. I tightened my choke hold and pressed my legs and back against the floor as I squeezed my arms together. We were locked together like this for what seemed like an eternity. His body shook violently. He thrashed about, his arms and hands trying to grab anything and pull or gouge and inflict pain and injury so that I would stop. I gave him nothing.

I held him in the tightest vice lock grip I'd ever managed, all my energy and focus zeroed in on this one mission—to strangle the life out of him and kill him here on my basement floor. Then I would do the same to Roberto.

There was no movement anywhere else in the room. I managed a short glance around as we fought, concerned Roberto might come to his senses, find and raise his shotgun or grab the handgun Fortunato had dropped when I hit him, and end it for me, Diane, and Chris. I was relieved to see he was still lying on the floor, barely moving—apparently in shock from the gunshot wound but certainly alive and possibly plotting his next move even as he lay there. My struggle with Fortunato was all consuming, and while I didn't have the luxury of being able to fully scan the room, this quick look showed no sign of either the handgun or that shotgun. I had to finish this and get to Roberto soon before he came to his senses, grabbed a gun and finished us first.

Fortunato continued to push against me, but I managed to stay on my side, thrusting my back even higher in the air. I quickly dropped my hips and back to the floor and swiveled, changing my position, bringing my legs around his full body, pinning both his arms and his legs in a wrestling move, while never losing my chokehold on his neck.

Chris and Diane both sat quietly in their chairs. Neither moved. Each was holding their breath, watching me with eyes wide open. An expression of shock, revulsion, and disbelief was on their faces. I was killing a man before their eyes. Choking the life out of him.

Chris's jaw was open, his eyes wide, and his face

expressionless. I was crushing the air—maybe the last bit of it—out of Fortunato. But even with my angle of vision narrowing as I struggled with and against Fortunato, I noticed two things around me; there was movement now across the room on the floor where Roberto was stirring, and Diane, although sitting perfectly still, now held Roberto's shotgun in her hands on her lap. The other shotgun rested on a table behind Chris, out of reach.

Thank god for small miracles.

Roberto was moving, roiling to one side, holding his badly damaged right arm with his other arm. That subtle change in the dynamic in the room was all it took for me to tighten my grip even more and for both Diane and Chris to turn their attention away from me and toward Roberto.

"Mom…"

The word was barely audible. Chris spoke with a quiet fear and dread. He had just met this man but that brief encounter was enough to teach him the immediate, mortal threat Roberto represented to him and his parents.

"Mom," he repeated, "he's getting up."

I heard the words and also knew well the threat they represented. I glanced over but was in no position to do anything about it. This man I held still had life and fight left in him. I had to finish him.

Diane's head had turned toward Roberto. She slowly raised the shotgun she had retrieved while I fought with Fortunato, opened it, looked inside, and snapped it back shut, confident it had the proper ammo to accomplish the nasty task at hand.

"Yeah, go ahead, make some sort of move, asshole," she said.

Diane's words were emotionless, spoken flatly, in a monotone voice and at a level just audible above the sounds of my struggle with Fortunato.

Roberto was making sounds, but the words were hard to make out. He rolled slowly onto one side and turned his head toward me.

Fortunato's gasps became more urgent, more frantic, and filled the room with an awful, horrible finality. The gulps of air shorter and less frequent. His fingers digging through my pants and into my legs, which pinned his arms, drawing blood. My grip around his neck never loosening.

"Fuck, you shot me!" Roberto spit the words out in anger and pain. "And you're killing Fortunato?" He said it with shock and horror.

He was awake and aware. Speaking slowly and quietly, but with disbelief—as if his own invincibility had also been proven false.

"I'm going to shoot you again in a minute," Diane sounded serious, and the shotgun didn't betray her words. It was aimed squarely at Roberto's body. "If you don't stop moving and shut the fuck up."

As he turned slowly around, his expression was more of a shrug of understanding. He was a quick study.

Diane, just five feet from him, had his loaded shotgun trained on him. A few feet past her, he watched as I choked the final bit of life out of his last remaining soldier. Chris sat wide-eyed in between. He was going to need years of therapy to get past this.

"What do you make of all this, young man?"

Roberto's ramblings amidst the murder and mayhem added even more crazy surrealism to the scene. How any of this could be happening in our home was beyond imagination.

"Don't fucking look at him, don't talk to him, and don't make a move or I'll pull the trigger," Diane said.

She had sensed Roberto's immediate sizing up of the situation—that he had concluded our son was the weakest link—a possible exposure point for us. She was right to think that. That's exactly how Roberto's brain worked.

If he could get to Chris somehow, he might have a fighting chance. What he really needed though, was that handgun lying by itself on the floor just a few feet away.

The last bit of life supporting air slipped out of Fortunato's lungs and past his lips. His body tensed up, went straight out rigid then released all that stiffness. A strange, quiet calm overcame him as his body went limp.

He lay there lifeless and still, yet I kept my tight grip around his throat for another minute, squeezing with all my might, just in case.

A wet, warm feeling enveloped me. Fortunato's bladder acknowledged his passing.

Everyone in the room seemed transfixed and was spellbound at the scene on the floor. Roberto's eyes were locked on mine as I finally released my grip and rolled Fortunato's dead body off me and onto the floor next to me.

"Not feeling so sure of yourself anymore, are you?" I asked Roberto.

I couldn't help myself. This was one of the few times in my interactions with Roberto when I actually felt like I might have the upper hand.

"What's the matter? Finally thinking maybe you're going to get what's coming to you after all these years? Worried it's the end of your run?"

I surprised myself with my boldness and ability to talk trash—let alone speak at all—after murdering a man with my bare hands.

"No," was all Roberto said after a tense, ten second pause in the conversation.

But I could tell that while he wasn't saying much, the wheels were spinning in his head. He was trying to find an angle. Any angle that would offer an escape from the deadly jam he now found himself in. I hadn't yet spotted the gun.

He brought his knees around in front of himself and perched himself on them, as if he were bracing himself and about to stand up.

"Stop moving Roberto," again, Diane was putting the warning out there in a slow, deliberate, serious tone. I don't think anyone in the room doubted she would pull the trigger.

"I was just thinking," he began, the words finally forming from the thoughts he seemed to have swirling in his head.

"Don't think," Diane's tone was serious, unemotional, and even. "And don't move."

Roberto stopped moving for the moment. Not making someone who has a gun pointed at you want to pull the trigger was a concept he believed in, Neverbut he hadn't stopped pondering his dilemma and he wasn't done talking. After a short pause, he continued.

"Diane, I understand how you feel, truly I do," this was the heartfelt, big brotherly, caring Roberto. But his words found no purchase in his intended target.

"No. You don't."

He breathed in and out—it was a big sigh—then, in what I thought was either stupidity or bravery, he continued.

"You're here because of a lie. Not my lie, but his lie," looking directly at me now.

"Lies, actually. Lies first to me in his actions all those years ago when he stole what belonged to me and took it to start a new life."

"Stop."

"And then, years later, lies to you. About the money, about the relationship you never knew about. About his past and the very man he said he was."

"Please… stop." The gun was still leveled at Roberto. Any more words falling from his lips might be all the pressure needed on the trigger for it to pull.

"And I'm sorry about that. Sorry you had to find out about it like you did. Sorry your son is here and hearing about it now. Sorry you're all dragged into this."

"I am going to shoot you." Both hands were on the gun now. Her right trigger finger was in place and her left hand now held the barrel. It was cocked and ready. I expected the thunderous report any second.

"Mom, don't." The words came from out of the blue.

Chris spoke slowly, quietly but urgently, surprising

Diane and me—but apparently not Roberto. It turned out that Chris was his intended target in this latest verbal assault, and he'd scored a bull's-eye.

Diane and I both looked at Chris, seemingly remembering as one that he was there. But Roberto had never forgotten. Chris was his ace in the hole. While Diane and I had worried about Roberto and Fortunato and the threat to our lives they represented, he had been contemplating Chris and the opportunity he presented. Roberto was certain Diane would not shoot him with her son watching.

And he was willing to bet his life on it.

"In my heart, I truly never wanted to hurt you Diane, or harm your son." Roberto picked his pitch, his plea, back up gingerly, hoping he hadn't overreached. Hoping Diane wouldn't pull the trigger. Betting on his ability as a manipulator and her maternal instincts over her anger. Betting that while she still held enough hatred inside her heart to kill him, her mother's compassion and fear of harming her son would prevent her from pulling the trigger and create the opportunity he needed to walk away from this alive.

He continued on.

"This was never about you. It was only about Dan. And it was about something that was solely between the two of us. I was wrong to have come here and pull you and your family into this. I see that clearly now and want to apologize for what I have done here. I'm sorry."

Diane's head tilted to the side as she watched Roberto

now, like a dog's head does when it doesn't understand the words being spoken to it.

Now the wheels were turning in her head. She wanted more than anything else to pull the trigger and lay Roberto out. Kill him and put an end to this insanity once and for all. Eliminate the threat to her family—her family's survival—and find a way to move past it.

But she had to calculate what that action would do to her young son's psyche. He'd already been taken hostage and held at gunpoint. Already seen her get assaulted and pushed around. Already seen his father get shot, and then, beyond anything he—or she—had ever imagined possible, watched along with her as I strangled a man to death with my bare hands.

Maybe shooting Roberto and killing him in front of Chris would be the best possible conclusion—but maybe not. Maybe it was something worth avoiding. Maybe finding a non-violent closure or one where the violence occurred elsewhere would be the less harmful thing to her son, whatever that could possibly be.

That was a lot of maybes.

She wished she were a man instead of a mother at this moment. Thoughts like these wouldn't be tormenting her. She would have pulled the trigger by now and sent Roberto to the hell he deserved.

"Diane."

It was my voice directed at her now, gentle but direct. It shook her from the odd trance she had put herself into. She blinked twice, wide-eyed and suddenly confused.

"He's playing you." I spoke slowly and clearly.

"He wants you to doubt. Wants you to hesitate. Wants your indecision. Wants you not to pull that trigger, no matter what happens. He wants the ability to grab that handgun on the floor and will do whatever he can to make that opportunity happen. And all these words he's spewing at you are just that, words. They are a smokescreen for his real intent, which is and always has been our total destruction and death."

As if on cue, she looked down at the floor and then back up to Roberto, then over to me and finally back to him. The handgun lay just out of his reach only a couple feet from where he knelt on the floor. If she hesitated—for the briefest of moments—he could lunge, grab it and shoot any one of us.

Looking at her with calm, pleasant eyes, and an expressionless face, Roberto said nothing. He was disappointed that we had spotted the handgun, but he'd already sown the seeds of doubt in her head.

My body ached. Blood continued to pulse from my bullet wound with the beat and rhythm of my heart, which was thundering and felt like it would gallop clear out of my chest from the life-threatening tension I felt coursing through my body.

"You control the situation Diane."

Roberto had decided that enough time for thoughtful reflection had passed.

"You control the situation and you control the outcome."

Roberto maintained his calm demeanor. Nothing about his tone, inflection or the very words were threatening. But everyone in the room knew his threat to their survival was real. Very real.

"Diane."

I needed her to pay attention to me, not to Roberto. I needed her to give me the shotgun.

"Give me the shotgun."

Roberto's expression changed ever so slightly. His brow furrowed just enough so that he gave away the slightest flash of concern. We both knew that I would pull the trigger and kill him as soon as I had my hands on it. Having Chris see me do it was not a concern for me and we both knew it. He'd just watched me strangle a man to death after all. Seeing me shoot Roberto was just one more thing for his soon to be hired therapist to work through with him.

Roberto continued to face Diane, but his eyes darted to me for the briefest of moments. As our eyes locked, we both knew one of us would soon be dead.

"Diane."

I said it calmly, but with a little more volume and a little more directness this time. I wanted to maintain the illusion of control and strength, but I was becoming worried. A new fear had taken hold.

I was losing blood quickly and eventually, possibly soon, I would black out. If that happened, it would be Diane and Roberto one on one and even with his mangled arm; I didn't care at all for those odds.

I needed to end this. Now.

Death resulting from the bullet wound was certainly a very real possibility, and I'd come to grips with that. While that wasn't desirable, it was acceptable if Diane and Chris survived and Roberto did not. What I hadn't thought through—until now—was that the bullet wound was a ticket to a slow death. More than likely, I'd eventually lose the strength and clarity that adrenaline was affording me now. And when that moment came, Roberto would strike.

"Give me the gun, Diane."

This time it was more of an order than a question or request. Roberto turned his full attention to me now. Chris too was looking at me, watching wide-eyed.

Diane appeared to be the only one in the room who didn't realize I wanted the shotgun, so I could kill Roberto and end this.

"Diane, don't do it."

It was Roberto's turn to pull at her emotions in our life and death game of tug of war. He knew his chances were slim to begin with but if I had the shotgun in my hands, his chances for survival would be eliminated completely.

"This man, your husband, is a liar. And as we've seen today, he's a killer."

"So are you."

It was all I could come up with.

Roberto sighed. This wasn't going to be easy, but his life depended on his ability to sow the seeds of doubt, create a diversion and get his hands on that damn handgun laying on the floor just beyond his grasp.

"I am that. I am not going to tell you I am not. I am both those things."

He had to think fast and remain motionless until movement was the only remaining option. And when that moment came, he had to be swift and sure.

"But I've known nothing else. All my life, from when I was a child younger than your boy here, violence surrounded me, and violence allowed me to survive."

"Diane," my voice began to show the first signs of weakness and despair.

"Oh poor, poor Roberto," Diane's voice was loud, roaring almost. She was listening to Roberto's every word but was she paying attention to me?

"Am I… are we… supposed to feel sorry for you, huh?"

She shook her head as she mockingly smirked at him.

"Sorry for *you*?" she continued.

"You're a cold-blooded killer. A drug dealer. Every awful thing you've done, you've done for your own personal wealth. Your own greed. My husband may have lied by keeping his past from me and my sons, but he did it for honest, noble reasons. He did it for us. It wasn't greed, it was love!"

There was anger and tremble in the tone and pitch of her blast. A bit of spit clung to her upper lip. The words were directed at Roberto but there was more than a little self-help bravado in her mini tirade too.

Roberto didn't show any of the frustration he surely felt inside. He did a good job of concealing his true emotions. His face was expressionless; even though I was sure her barbs had found their mark. They had to have.

Desperation was not mine alone after all, but it was hard to tell just by looking at him.

"You can sell it any way you want to Diane." Roberto picked up the conversation calmly—as if it were one, after the shortest of pauses.

"But he lied. And as we all just saw, he killed. That makes him…" he paused for effect."

"A liar and a killer."

"A liar and a killer." He repeated it for impact. "Whatever his reasons, he's no better than me."

Roberto could take bullets and barbs and come back throwing roundhouses.

Diane was stunned by his words and the numbing impact they had on her. She looked at me as if to confirm or deny what he'd said. Chris was staring at him, shaking. I felt my strength and my life seeping away. Roberto was beginning to see a crack that could create an opening for him to make a grab for the gun.

"He's a killer and a liar." Roberto continued, smelling blood in the water, he went in deeper.

"I know you love him—I know you both love him," he looked at her, then at Chris.

"I'm not trying to talk you out of that. I get that. I understand."

He was looking back and forth at us all now. One by one, making individual eye contact as if he were talking to us with our best interests at heart, not his. He was selling— marketing—a new plan. It was the "I'm not as bad a guy as you might think when you look at the bigger picture" sell. The story where he can't help being the way he is, and he should be forgiven and allowed to be the way he is. Allowed to walk away from this.

"You love him, and you should. He's no doubt been a good husband and father. But he's faulted. It's only natural, we all are."

Now it was therapist Roberto. He hadn't survived this long being a one trick pony drug lord.

"I am faulted too. Terribly faulted. Dan knows this."

He looked at me and nodded, as if I was in on the story he was spinning.

"How else could I have held a grudge like this for so many years? Why would I have?"

Diane and Chris appeared to be hypnotized by him.

Against my better judgment, I sat spellbound too, listening to a story I knew in my heart was utter bullshit.

"I can see now I was wrong. The vindictive hatred I brought here, the violence I brought here—to your family, in your home, was uncalled for. I am sorry."

The words behaved like some strange nerve blocking agent, severing the tie between our brains and our tongues.

We were staring at him in confused disbelief for what seemed like an eternity but in reality, was more likely a mere ten seconds. He certainly hadn't grown less timid over the years.

"Sorry? That's the best you got?" I had finally snapped myself out of his bullshit induced haze.

"Yes Dan, I'm sorry. I apologize."

"Really?"

"Yes. I am sorry. And I would like it very much if you would forgive me and allow me to leave."

"Do I look crazy?" Diane and Chris sat expressionless, watching us banter. Neither reacted to his wildly bold request nor my disbelieving reaction to it.

"I understand your hesitancy. You know me Dan. I am stubborn, and bull headed, but I am also a man of my word. I give you my word now that if you allow me to leave, I will not come back, and I will not harm you."

Diane's sudden, somber quietness hinted to me what I feared—that she was being sucked into believing him. And why not? It was a plea for sanity amidst the chaos. It could end this now without any more violence, death, and trauma.

"Diane, look at me." She turned toward me. Her face was blank, expressionless.

"I do know this man. Or at least, I did all those years ago. He was a violent, sadistic man, who never stopped until he had what he wanted. Was he a man of his word? Sure, but I never knew that word to be a plea for nonviolence or compassion. We cannot believe him. You cannot believe him. He will kill us regardless of what he is saying now."

Roberto was not going to allow that claim to go uncontested.

"I know you are strong, couragcous, and graceful Diane. Allow me to leave and I promise you…" Roberto was continuing on, hoping he could convince them of the lie he told so convincingly—that they could stop all this right now and end this forever.

"Fuck off!" Diane finally shouted at him, cutting him off mid-sentence.

"I promise you…" he continued, still calmly, undeterred.

"Fuck off!"

This time, she yelled it louder without any hesitation and brought the shotgun up. She'd heard enough.

"Diane, don't."

I was surprised the words came from me and not Roberto.

It was less than a shout, but it was all I could immediately muster. I thought for sure she was going to pull the trigger right then and there. I wasn't sure why I yelled it because pulling the trigger was what needed to be done. Maybe Roberto's impassioned plea to not kill him in front of Chris had found its mark on me. I was walking a fine line between wanting him dead and not wanting my son to see his mother be the one who killed him. Why that mattered was beyond me.

Diane and Roberto stared at each other. Her eyes, which had seconds ago seemed to have been vacant, now were ablaze in hatred. Her finger twitched on the trigger of the shotgun. All she had to do was squeeze.

"I promise YOU," she said finally, staring through to what she thought might have been his soul.

"If I have to, I'll pull this trigger and end this once and for all right now. Enough of your bullshit. I believe Dan, not you. You'll say anything to get yourself out of this jam you're in here. But here's the thing—I'm not buying it. Not buying any of it."

They looked deep into each other's eyes. Neither spoke. Diane was back, grounded, where I needed her to be. I just needed her to be settled enough so that she could get that handgun on the floor and give it to me. Then she and Chris could get out of this room and call the police and I could finish our business with Roberto before they arrived.

"Mom?" Chris was looking at Roberto but talking to his mother. He was scared. Shit, everyone left alive in the room was scared.

"Chris honey, please stay out of this." But he was in this. He'd literally been dragged off the street and into this insane, desperate carnival.

"Mom," he continued, ignoring her.

"Don't shoot him, please." He was begging in a quiet, scared, sincere voice.

"Honey, this is a bad man who came here to kill your dad. He was probably going to kill me too. But not before he and his men did awful things to me."

"I believe you," he said, now looking at his mother.

"I just can't see that. I don't want to see that."

And there it was, Roberto's marketing plan had found the one mark in the room it needed to and now had a committed customer. The most important customer.

She didn't take her eyes of Roberto as she talked in a firm, calm tone to her youngest boy. Her baby.

"I know, honey, I know."

She sighed and continued.

"But this bad man won't be stopped by us just asking him to, no matter what he says he will do."

"Isn't that right?" Diane said this to Roberto, but she didn't wait for his response and continued on to Chris.

"We're only alive right now because we fought back.

That man sitting right there talking so calmly to us right now was prepared to kill you just a couple of minutes ago, honey. But probably not until after he and that other horrible man tortured you or made you watch as they tortured and killed me or your dad."

"Can't we just call the cops?"

"Or both." Diane finished her sentence as if she hadn't even heard her son's plea.

In a sane world, Chris's request made complete sense. Hold the gun on the bad guy, call the good guys, wait for them to arrive and put the bad guy in jail. But the world Chris had stumbled into this afternoon was more like the Wild West than the suburban Pittsburgh he'd grown up in and was accustomed to—the one he lived in as recently as this morning.

"So, no honey, we aren't going to call the cops. That's not how this works. That's not how this is going to go down."

Diane's defiance and strength had the opposite effect of helping me and giving me strength. Her words were a weight on my shoulders and heart that seemed unnaturally heavy.

I could feel my own strength and will to fight ebbing away. I was losing blood. I was in shock. How was this going to go down? Did Diane have a plan? We were going to need one if she wasn't going to shoot Roberto right now because somebody was going to have to put another bullet in him and that somebody was me.

For god's sake, I had to find a way to bring this to a resolution as quickly as possible, while I still had most my strength and faculties. While I was still able to make an impact and control the situation. While I was still conscious.

I needed that gun in my hands and my wife and kid out of that room.

Every minute wasted talking was one where I lost a little more blood, a little more strength.

Diane continued, "That's why we're going to have to settle things here, just between the four of us."

Diane never let her eyes drift from Roberto's. She was playing with him now. Playing with his emotions and with his psyche. She wanted to shake him, take him off the offense for once in his drug dealing, scumbaggy life and make him think his fate was not in his own hands.

By the smile he managed to keep steady and straight, it was hard to determine if he was shaken in the least. He kept his eyes clear and focused on hers. If there was doubt, fear or uncertainty in his head or heart, no one in the room knew it for sure except for him.

I'd seen Roberto back in the day when he was a tough guy in tough spots, and I'd seen a lot of movies about ill-tempered drug dealers—many of which could have had Roberto's real-life personality starring in them. The characteristics those men presented to the world—the young Roberto and the Hollywood drug dealer—were presented here to us in this room in the bravado and persona of present-day Roberto.

I had no doubt that this man here before us would say or do anything that would give him the slightest advantage possible, so that he could get whatever it is he wanted or needed. He would do whatever it took—and in the end, he would act as he always did in the end—as a vicious, soulless, violent animal. This front he presented to us now was just an act. I prayed Diane really did understand this and wasn't acting or bluffing herself out of a position of control.

Chapter 26

"I want nothing more than to settle this," Roberto said. After sitting in silence, listening to and judging Diane's conviction, Roberto had decided it was his turn to talk, his turn to act.

He was slowly unfastening his belt. He pulled it off as we watched and made a loop out if it, bringing his bleeding right arm through it. He was slowly bleeding to death, too.

"Without any more violence. Without any more death." He continued talking while he tightened the belt loop around his arm. He was in bad shape—maybe as bad as me.

He began to stir, slowly rising onto his knees. And then, as if delivering a warning…

"I would like to stand up."

"No!" Dianc and I said in unison.

He stopped. He sat forward on his knees. His left hand was perched on his thigh. His right hand held the length of his belt—it stretched out a foot and a half or more from his hand, which was covered in blood.

"Please. I am unarmed and pose no threat. You hold a shotgun pointed at me."

"Stay where you are." Diane said it slowly and sternly.

"I represent no further threat to you. To any of you."

I stared at him, not believing he had the nerve to try something with a gun held on him.

"I would like to stand up, slowly." He repeated it, and then did what he said, to mine and Diane's disbelief.

Slowly, deliberately and eventually, Roberto began to rise to his feet. The threat level in the room was a ten out ten.

"You need to sit back down," Diane was imploring him to listen and stop any further movement, but Roberto was having none of it.

"Then, I am going to walk slowly to that door," pointing to the sliding door that lead from our finished basement to our backyard and the woods beyond. Yesterday, he and his men had spied on my house and my family from those very woods.

"I am going to open that door and walk out into your yard, find my car, and leave this place."

"Roberto, I can't allow that happen."

The words were mine. I spoke them calmly and clearly. I knew that if he left, no matter what he said now, he would come back to kill me, to kill us all, probably with even more men and guns, and fewer inhibitions. Not today, unless he had more men tucked away someplace close that we were unaware of. But someday. And likely, someday soon. This thing would not be over. It had lived on for decades. This dust up would not be the end. It wouldn't be over until Roberto said it would be—and that wouldn't be until my family and I were all dead.

I wished I held a gun in my hand. I knew I could—and would—pull the trigger. I didn't know what Diane would do as push came to shove and the only thing left that would stop Roberto was a bullet.

"This can end now, Diane," he stood there now, just feet from her, intending to do as he said, and walk out our basement door.

"It can end here."

"Mom?" Chris was frightened. There was no way for him to know just how right he was to feel that afraid. He needed assurances this would somehow be OK. We didn't have any answers for him but Diane and I both felt his urgent need and turned our attention to him in that brief instant.

It was the opening Roberto had been waiting for.

He spun around in a near full circle. The swiftness and urgency of his movements at direct odds with the calm demeanor and bantering he had been engaged in. His arm sprayed blood out in front of it as it swung around. The leather belt was extended fully and acted like a whip as it struck the shotgun.

Wack!

Diane was caught completely by surprise. She put all of her strength and energy into hanging on to the shotgun. It was nearly ripped from her hands. She grabbed at it, tightening her grip in desperation. Her finger pulled the trigger and it discharged its second and final shell in a thunderous blast into the wall.

The sound wave hit me like a punch, reverberating through my entire body, stopping all motion and thought.

Diane sat shocked, holding her empty, useless shotgun, staring wide-eyed and mouth open at Roberto.

He wasn't the least bit shocked. It was his plan after all. He was still moving, closing the space between him and the handgun. We'd all be dead in seconds if I couldn't get there and stop him.

The adrenaline was back, kicking in instantaneously, lurching me thoughtless and violently through the air toward him. This was it. It was all I had left in my tank.

He was on it now, grabbing at the handgun like it was a carnival prize. I was moving in fast and hard, but I wasn't there. I hadn't reached him in time.

He spun around so quickly, it was as if he were not bound by the laws of physics.

How could he take a bullet and behave like this?

The last thing I remember seeing before the blast, was the look in Roberto's eyes. Wild, animalistic, and happily victorious. I hadn't reached him in time. Victory was his.

The gunshot was incredibly loud. But I was confused. I expected to see the muzzle flash brightly, just inches from my face. I expected to feel the awful searing heat as the bullet tore through me and extinguished my life. But I saw and felt none of that.

Instead, Roberto exploded before me and on me. Warm blood—his—shot out at me from his neck and chest at the same time he was seemingly pushed violently backward through the air. Blood and guts—his—were everywhere. The gun he would have used to kill me, my wife, and son dropped harmlessly and hit the floor at exactly the same instant Roberto's body did.

The gunshot had come from behind me. I turned and saw Chris, standing there, holding a still smoking shotgun in his hands. The shotgun Fortunato had laid on the table. The expression on his face was part hatred, part fear. He was sure of his action but didn't like it just the same.

My son had done what he had begged his mother not to do. Roberto was dead. It was over.

Chapter 27

A case of mistaken identity is what we told the police when they arrived. We didn't know these men who came to torture and kill us. They spoke with foreign accents and talked about drugs and money—which we knew nothing about. Once they realized they had the wrong house and people, they changed their plan to one of robbing and murdering us. It was only through sheer determination—and luck—that we managed to overpower them, turn the guns on them and kill them before they murdered us. In the epic struggle that ensued, I was badly injured, and my wife and son were traumatized.

The police were skeptical—it was a story that made sense only on the surface. But I was an upstanding citizen with political ties and a spot free track record, including police donations. They hadn't bothered to examine my financial records close enough to find the offshore account I had created just days ago. Amazingly, Roberto carried a wallet with his actual Florida license in it. He was quickly identified and once the authorities knew who was lying dead in a pool of blood on my basement floor, we were no longer the center of the investigation or attention.

Things happened fast once all that came together. Police in Pittsburgh and Miami conferred with the FBI. Warrants were issued to search Roberto's home on the beach as well as open all his bank accounts to their forensic investigators. Piece by piece they quickly put their own version of the truth together. Thanks to us, police had stumbled upon one of the largest, most successful drug traffickers in the country. Through a quirk of fate, he was neutralized, and his entire network was now exposed and would soon be closed. I was in surgery when the authorities issued their congratulatory statements to the media.

We moved into temporary housing while contractors ripped up floors and carpeting and remodeled the areas destroyed by Roberto and his thugs. Our family single handedly increased the workload of Pittsburgh area therapists by tenfold—my wife and I both had therapists we saw individually as well as a marriage counselor—all working to help me make sense out of my past and our future and to put us back together. Trust had to be rebuilt. The boys both needed help as well. The therapists all agreed a long family vacation would give us the time and setting to be open and honest with each other and would give Diane and the kids a chance to get to know me—the real me—something I embraced and was relieved to have the opportunity to do.

One of the therapists suggested Florida as a vacation spot—we all agreed we'd rather go someplace else.

Bob Longo was born and raised in Upstate New York. After college, he worked as a reporter – first in Radio, then TV. Eventually, he decided being the boss was better than having a bad one, and he became a News Director. Fortunately, the bosses he had during those years were mostly exceptional. He spent much of his career running TV newsrooms in Jacksonville, Orlando, Pittsburgh and Buffalo. He is currently the General Manager of the CBS & FOX TV stations in Jacksonville, Florida. He's married to his college sweetheart, Laurie. They have two sons, Nicholas and Alexander and are lucky to also have a faithful, furry friend, Luna. He's told plenty of stories during his long career and heard even more. Boomerang Bandito is unlike any of those.

www.ingramcontent.com/pod-product-compliance
Lightning Source LLC
Chambersburg PA
CBHW022034240626
47154CB00007B/2396